Plain and Simple

Robert Bailey

Writers Club Press
San Jose New York Lincoln Shanghai

Plain and Simple

Published by Writers Club Press
an imprint of iUniverse.com, Inc.

For information address:
iUniverse.com, Inc.
620 North 48th Street
Suite 201
Lincoln, NE 68504-3467
www.iuniverse.com

ISBN: 0-595-09329-9

Printed in the United States of America

Chapter 1

6:00 a.m. Sunday
Jan. 2, 2000

The wind driven rain beat down on the asphalt parking lot so hard and fast, it flooded the storm drain and backed up nearly six inches deep around the cars parked in the back stalls. The rain came down as sleet at times. It was almost cold enough to turn into snow.

Two Pueblo police cruisers sat near the back door of the large motel, their red strobe lights reflecting off the salmon colored walls of the five-story building. A four door Ford Crown Vic came down the street, the tires throwing a spray as they plowed through the water flowing along the curbs. It slowed for the driveway and turned into the motel parking lot. The driver pulled into an empty stall near the back door, turned off the lights and killed the motor. He reached into the back seat, looking for a raincoat. He struggled putting it on in the confined space of the front seat, opened the door and walked the short distance to the motel. A uniformed patrol officer opened the door for him.

"Good morning sergeant," the officer greeted him. "Room 223 toward the back."

The sergeant nodded and went through the door. He walked to the lobby, past the desk to the elevators, pushed the button to go up and stepped in when the doors opened. He stepped out into the hallway on the second floor, and then walked to the patrol officer standing outside the second room from the end of the building.

The patrol officer was over six feet, weighing two hundred pounds plus. He wasn't fat. He was big. His weight covered a large framed body and his uniform fit very well, as though tailored. His dark black hair was neatly trimmed, his face was rugged and he may have been considered handsome when he was younger, but time had etched lines around the eyes and down across his cheeks. His nose was bent and crooked from previous fights, and white scars covered his cheekbones. He was full-blooded Apache or was it Arapaho. None of his peers knew what tribe he was. No one had the nerve to ask.

"Piss poor way to start a Sunday morning Jerry," he said, greeting the sergeant. He was the only patrolman that didn't defer to the sergeant's rank. He always addressed him by his given name.

"Good morning to you too, Red Bear. What do you have?" the sergeant said.

Officer James Red Bear opened the door to room 223 and went inside. The sergeant followed, preparing himself for the first look at the body of the latest homicide victim.

"The last person on this earth you would expect. It's our local county sheriff, Orville Boone," Red Bear said as the sergeant caught sight of the man lying on the bed.

"Holy Shit! Have you called everyone?" the sergeant said as he moved closer to the bed.

"Only you. I figured this was not going to be just a run of the mill case," Red Bear told him.

The man on the bed was dressed in a one-piece suit of long underwear. He was somewhere in his late fifties, skinny build, balding head and when alive would have been described as having a ruddy complexion, resulting from years of heavy drinking. There was a small splotch of blood on the underwear over his heart and a small dark colored hole in his forehead, just above his right eye.

"Who called it in?" the sergeant asked.

"Night clerk. He said the sheriff called down around ten last night and left a request for a wake up call at 5:30. He tried several times with no answer. He came up here, used his pass key and found him."

"The first shot was in the forehead, that's why there is little blood?"

"That's how I figure it," Red Bear responded. "The one in the heart wasn't necessary. The shooter just added one for his own reason, whatever that might be."

"Call Lieutenant Winters, the coroner and our detail people," the sergeant told him.

Red Bear pulled on a pair of thin rubber gloves and picked up the phone. He made the first call, and then held out the receiver for the sergeant.

"Is it really Orville Boone?" he heard the voice of Lieutenant Winters ask.

"It's him boss. Someone put two in him sometime between ten last night and five thirty this morning," the sergeant responded.

"Where are you?" the lieutenant asked.

"The Holiday Inn where I-25 runs into Highway 50."

"A motel. What in the hell was he doing in a motel?"

"Don't know yet."

"Well seal it up tight. No press. I'll be out there as soon as I can get dressed," the lieutenant said. The sergeant handed the phone back to Red Bear to make the other calls.

Sergeant Jerico Magee went around the bed and pulled the drapes open. The dark clouds and rain obscured the view from the window, as it hammered on the glass. He pulled a chair away from the table and sat down, took a pack of cigarettes from his shirt pocket and lit one. He fished around in his inside jacket pocket for a small notebook and put it on the table. He sat looking all around the motel room. The sheriff's pants were on the floor by the bed, his shoes near the pants. His shirt was on one corner of the bottom of the bed. A coat hung on the single bar attached to the wall by the door. What in the hell were you doing in this place on new years day, Magee asked in his mind, looking at the stiff body on the bed.

"Everyone's on the way. Want me to go talk to the clerk for a statement?" Red Bear asked.

"No, I'll do it. Sit on the room until the forensics people show," Magee said.

He left the chair and went out of the room, found the stairs and walked down one flight and came out in the lobby. He went to the desk, around behind and into a room used as an office. A young man barely twenty stood talking to a heavyset woman sitting at a desk.

"Good morning. I'm Sergeant Magee, Pueblo Homicide. Are you the one who found the body in 223?" he asked the young man.

"Yes. I didn't know he was dead at first. I thought he was just sleeping off a drunk," he said.

"What's your name?"

"Myron. Myron Reed."

"You been working here long Myron?"

"Two months. I go to school during the week and work here on weekends. The third shift. Nine to five."

"Who rented the room?"

"The sheriff. He has been here before when he has too much to drink. He evidently didn't want to drive drunk or didn't want to go home," the woman volunteered.

"What's your name?" Magee asked her.

"Sharlotte Reese. I work the day shift."

"What time did the sheriff check in?"

"9:52 P.M. according to the computer," she responded.

"Were you here?"

"No, Myron was on duty."

"Was the sheriff alone, Myron?"

"Yes."

"Was he intoxicated?"

"Very much so."

"Did anyone come in after he did, asking for him or his room number?"

"There were several guests. Some checked in. Some were already registered and just went by the desk. No one asked for the sheriff," Myron responded.

"Did you notice anyone out of the ordinary?"

"What do you mean?"

"Anyone who looked suspicious or acted strange?"

"Not that I noticed."

"Did the sheriff make any phone calls?"

"I wouldn't know. He could call from the room without going through the switchboard down here."

Magee saw several men coming into the lobby, water running off their rain wear.

"Why don't you go on home Myron and get some sleep. When you get up later, come down to police headquarters and we'll type up a statement for you to sign," the sergeant said. Without waiting for a response, he went out and around the desk.

"Room 232 and toward the back," he told the forensics people. He was about to follow them upstairs when his boss, Chief of Detectives Lieutenant Aaron Winters and the police chief came through the front door. The chief was dressed in an expensive, suit as he usually was. Winters looked like he slept in his clothes.

"What in the hell was Boone doing in here. Did he have a skirt on the side?" the chief asked. Chief Daniel Morrison had been the head of the police department for twelve years and had survived through four different city administrations.

"The clerk said he had a habit of stopping here on the nights he had too much to drink. Probably to stay away from his wife," Magee said.

"The D.A. is on his way Jerry," Lieutenant Winters said. "Wait for him and bring him up." He and the chief crossed to the elevators and pushed the button for a car. The door had just closed on them when Walter Sugden, the district attorney came through the back door of the lobby. If Jerry Magee had one friend in Pueblo it had to be Walt Sugden. They were close to the same age. Neither was married and both spent too much time on the job.

"Who would want to whack Orville Boone?" the D.A. asked.

"I just got here Walt. I'm going to need a little time before I can answer," Magee responded.

"Show me where he is?" Sugden said.

"Room 232," Magee said as he led the D.A. to the elevators.

As the elevator doors closed, Magee saw the other two detectives of the homicide squad come through the front door. He smiled as he saw their faces. Neither of them appeared very pleased to be out in a rainstorm on a Sunday morning. Homicide consisted of the lieutenant, himself, Sergeant Donald Stone and Sergeant Andy Rehaus. Magee wasn't surprised to see them here. He figured the lieutenant called them in. He would want everybody working on this one.

He led the D.A. down to the room, which was rapidly becoming crowded. He stood out in the hall waiting for the other two sergeants.

"So, you were up for this one Magee. Why do you need us?" Sergeant Stone asked.

"I didn't call. Who called?" Magee asked.

"Dispatch said the lieutenant wanted us here," Sergeant Rehaus volunteered. "It's your case. What do you want us to do?"

"Check DMV for what the sheriff drives, then look for it down in the parking lot."

"Why not call the sheriff's office and ask?" Stone said.

"Because the chief and the lieutenant haven't given the word to make the notifications yet. You want to go in there and tell them how you want to do this one?" Magee asked him.

Stone didn't respond. He turned around and went down the hallway, Rehaus right behind him.

The chief, Winters and the D.A. came out of the room. Winters moved to the front of the three, giving Magee orders.

"Notify the chief deputy over at the sheriff's office. After the coroner leaves, you get to notify Mrs. Boone. I called Stone and Rehaus in to help on this one. Keep us up to date and be sure Walter knows what's going on," the lieutenant said. He and the chief went down in the elevator.

"There's a cafe on the other end of the motel," Magee told the D.A. "You hungry?"

"That sounds like an offer to buy. Lead the way," Sugden told him.

They walked down the fire stairs and across the lobby to the cafe. A young woman took them to a booth.

"You don't have to be upstairs?" the D.A. asked.

"Just be in the way. Forensics and the coroner have to do their thing first. Everything in the room will be recorded. I go to work when they're finished," Magee responded.

Stone and Rehaus appeared in the doorway, spotted them and came to the table. Stone was about to pull out a chair when the sergeant spoke to him.

"No car in the lot?"

"Nothing. DMV says he drives a year old Cadillac as his personal car. We won't know what county car he drove until we can check with his office," Stone said.

"The lieutenant just gave the okay. Call the chief deputy and notify them of his demise. When they're finished upstairs, ask if they found a gun. I didn't see any," Magee said.

"He didn't carry one," the D.A. responded.

"He didn't carry a gun! Why not?" Rehaus asked.

"He worked very hard to stay away from any violence. Always sent his deputies to do the hard work. He was an administrator only," Sugden told them.

"Well violence sure as hell caught up with him in the end," Stone said, smiling as though he had really said something. He was about to say something about sitting down for breakfast when Rehaus pulled on his arm and led him out of the cafe.

"That one is a slob," the D.A. said, referring to Stone.

"Among other things," the sergeant added.

Their breakfast was served and they started eating. The rain was still heavy, the dark sky holding back the morning light.

"You are aware the sheriff was dirty," Sugden said.

"From what I hear. How come you and I never talked about that?" Magee said.

"My office has looked into it several times over the years. We came up with nothing. Boone was smarter than he looked. How long have you been here?" Sugden asked.

"Six or seven months."

"What do you know about the sheriff's department?"

"Almost nothing. What little we have worked on with them always involved a deputy coming to us. I never met the sheriff. I've never been in the sheriff's office," the sergeant responded.

They finished eating and he walked Sugden to the back door of the motel. He left him with the promise to keep him up to date. Sugden hurried through the rain to his car and drove off.

Magee went back up to the room. As he came off the elevator, the coroner's people were bringing the body down the hall. He held the door on the elevator and they wheeled him in and went down. He went to room 223 where Red Bear, Stone and Rehaus were the only officers still there. The forensics people had taken all of Boone's clothing and personal items in. He sent Stone and Rehaus to the sheriff's office to go through his desk, when they left he walked through the room with Red Bear.

"Call down and get a patrolman to sit on the door for a while. You can go with me to notify the widow. What do you make of this?" Magee asked.

"The clerk said he comes here to sleep off too much liquor. No sign of forced entry. Both shots up close with powder residue very evident. They said his car is not down in the lot. I don't believe anything we have so far amounts to a pile of goose shit," Red Bear responded.

"You always have a way with words. Do you know where the sheriff lived?" Magee asked him.

"Big ranch house south on I-25," Officer Red Bear responded.

They went down the elevator and out to the parking lot in back. The storm was breaking up the rain had almost stopped.

"Let's go in your car since you know where we are going," Magee said as he got into Red Bear's police cruiser. Red Bear turned off the red lights and drove out of the lot and onto the interstate highway. He kicked the car up to the seventy and they were soon past the city limits. Ten minutes later, Red Bear slowed for an off ramp and turned onto an asphalt county road, heading east. Three miles further, he slowed for a driveway, and then turned right.

Magee was surprised at the house. Red Bear said it was a large ranch style house. It was certainly large. It sat back from the road two hundred yards, with an asphalt drive lined with large trees leading up to the front door. The place was worth two to three hundred thousand Magee thought.

"Was the sheriff a rich man?" he asked Red Bear.

"He was an asshole. Don't know if he was a rich asshole or not!" Red Bear said.

"What?" Magee said in surprise at the response.

"He treated his help like dirt. All the contact I had was with the patrol deputies. They all hated him," Red Bear told him.

"That's just great. You just added more suspects to the list. Stop by the front door there," Magee told him. They got out of the car and walked the few steps to the door. Before they could ring the bell, an attractive middle age woman opened the door.

"Mrs. Boone, I'm Sergeant Magee and this is Officer Jimmy Red Bear. We're with the Pueblo police department," Magee said.

"Is he dead?" the woman asked.

"What?" Magee responded, shocked by her greeting.

"Is the son of a bitch dead. I figured it had to be something like that to bring the city police out here," she said.

"May we come in?" Magee asked her.

"Sure. You didn't answer me," she said holding the door open for them.

They walked into the house and turned to her as she shut the door.

"Your husband was shot and killed sometime during the night," Magee said.

"Was he in that hotel?" she asked.

"He was in a room at the Holiday Inn north of Pueblo," he responded.

"That is not a big surprise sergeant. He had half a dozen places he took his floozies," she said.

"Pardon me!"

"Orville had two weaknesses sergeant. One was drinking too much booze; the other was trying to screw every hooker in Colorado. He suffered from the delusion that he was twenty years old and a stud in the pasture full of mares. You won't see me shed a tear for the bastard. I say good riddance," she said.

"Can you think of anyone with a particular grudge or reason to kill him?" Magee asked her.

"You'll find very few people who didn't want to kill him sergeant. There will be so many suspects they will have to take a number and get in line," she said. "Can I get you boys some coffee?"

"No thanks. The coroner's office has his body. When they are finished, they will call about an undertaker," Magee said.

"There's one in the city I went to school with. I'll just call him and tell him to pick up Orville and arrange some kind of a funeral. It won't be much. We had no kids and there is little family out here. No sir, won't be a big deal," she said.

They conveyed their condolences and left the widow, going back out to the car.

"That is one tough old bird," Red Bear said as he started the car and backed around to head out.

"That's an understatement. The question that comes to mind was why did she stay with him?" Magee said. "I was so shocked I forgot to ask about the sheriff's Cadillac. I think this will be a good item for Stone and Rehaus to follow up on."

Red Bear pushed the car up to seventy and the trip back into the city was brief. He drove back to the motel where Magee picked up his car, then followed Red Bear to police headquarters.

They parked behind an old two story brick building, Red Bear waiting for Magee to catch up, and then went up the few steps to the back door. They walked down a narrow hallway to the counter that fenced off the entryway by the front door. Standing behind the counter, reading a newspaper, was Sergeant Patrick Lopez, a heavy set, fifty year old duty sergeant that pulled one shift as watch commander of the uniform patrolman. From the first day he met Magee, he had sparred with him verbally. Magee found out this was common to all the police personnel that came and went in front of the sergeant's desk.

"Now I think it is terrible that a smart Jewish boy such as yourself should have to work on a Sunday, sergeant," Lopez greeted Magee. "And I see you have Crazy Horse working along side. Nothing good will come from that you know!"

"And a good morning to you sergeant. You know damn good and well that I wouldn't know what the inside of a Synagogue even looks like. And this kind of treatment I get from a man who doesn't know if he is Irish or Mexican," Magee responded.

"Now don't be saying anything bad about my ethnic mix, I am proud to be part of both. The only one in this station house that is one hundred percent something is Crazy Horse there," Lopez responded.

Red Bear said nothing. He was never baited by the sergeant's banter. He walked on by the desk and started up the old creaking steps to the second floor. Magee followed him, a smile on his face. Lopez was respected and well liked by all the uniform patrolman in the department.

Magee went to his office. Red Bear went to a desk he used with other patrolman, sat down and started on his report.

The phone on Magee's desk rang as he sat down in his chair.

"Have you made the notification to the widow?" Lieutenant Winters asked him.

"Just got back. She took it pretty well I would say. No love lost there," Magee responded.

"The chief wants this one closed soon. Do what you have to. Any word on his car yet?"

"We put an APB out on it. Did you know the sheriff?"

"Not very well. He was an odd individual. He seemed to shun everyone in our department. Find his killer," the lieutenant said then hung up.

Magee started his paper work on the case and was busy until after lunch.

Stone and Rehaus came into his office. Stone was picking his teeth, a sure sign he hadn't missed his lunch. Stone was at least thirty pounds overweight. He plopped down in a chair.

"What now. We canvassed the motel. No one saw anything?" Stone said.

"Take a ride out to the widow's place and look in the garage. Maybe the Cadillac is there," Magee said.

"I thought you went out there to notify her?" Stone responded.

"I did, but I didn't look in the garage," Magee told him.

"They found the car in Colorado Springs," Red Bear said as he came into the office. "The city cops picked up a kid driving it. They impounded the vehicle and have the driver in jail. Some detective just called dispatch."

"Did he leave his name?" Magee asked.

"I wrote it down," Red Bear said handing him a note. Magee handed it to Stone.

"Why don't you two run up there and have a talk with this kid. If it comes to anything, call the D.A. for a warrant," Magee said.

Stone started to protest, saw the look on Magee's face, took the note and left with Rehaus behind him.

"I'm off, you want anything from me?" Red Bear asked.

"Thanks for the help, see you tomorrow," Magee said.

"No you won't. Monday and Tuesday are my days off this week."

"See you Wednesday then," Magee said as Red Bear left his office.

Magee followed him out and downstairs, past the desk and out the back door. He pulled the collar of his coat up around his neck as he crossed the parking lot.

The wind had picked up again, the sky overcast and dark. The temperature was down close to thirty degrees. He drove across town to the small house he rented, parked in the driveway and went inside.

The house had been built in the fifties as part of a new subdivision. It had two small bedrooms, a kitchen, living room and a small bathroom. Magee had checked with a realtor when he moved to Pueblo and the house was one of several rentals the man owned personally. The rent wasn't bad and it even had some furniture in it.

He found some cold cuts in the refrigerator, made a sandwich and drank a beer as he ate. When he finished it was two thirty. He stretched out on the well-worn couch and went to sleep. He would sleep through the night.

Chapter 2

9:00 a.m. Monday
Jan. 3, 2000

Walter Sugden, district attorney for Pueblo County, sat at his large expensive desk in the Pueblo county courthouse, sipping on a fresh cup of coffee. Across the desk sat the chairman of the Pueblo County board of supervisors.

"I appreciate you taking the time to come over for coffee and a little conversation," the D.A. said.

"When you called and wanted to hear what we planned to do about the vacancy in the sheriff's office, I sure as hell couldn't refuse. This affects you too," the chairman responded.

"What do you and the board plan on doing?"

"The term isn't up for two years. We can call for a special election or appoint someone for the next two years," the chairman said.

"Is there someone in the department you might have in mind to appoint?" the D.A. asked him.

"I talked to the chief deputy. She doesn't want it. I asked her about any of the other deputies. She didn't suggest anyone. Get to it Walter."

"There is a sergeant in homicide on the Pueblo police department who would make a damn good sheriff. His name is Jerico Magee," the D.A. said.

"Never heard of him. How long has he been here?" the chairman asked.

"Just a few months. He spent twenty years in the army. He retired a major, got a job with the Denver police department. Went through the necessary training. Danny Morrison hired him away from them. He's thirty-seven, not married. He is an only child. His parents divorced while he was in the army. His father is deceased now. His mother lives in Omaha, Nebr. He was a captain in Special Forces during the gulf war, in command of a company. Received the usual decorations and commendations. The police chief says good things about him," the D.A. said.

"Thirty seven and not married! How come?"

"He's not gay if that's what you're asking. I don't know why he is not married. I think he has what you need to clean up the sheriff's department and get those people on the same page as the rest of us. If you are interested, I'll do some background checking and get you a report," the D.A. said.

"Will he take the job?" the chairman asked.

"Ask him and find out," he responded.

"Get me the background material. If he's interested, set up an appointment this week," the chairman said. He stood up to leave. "Any idea yet who killed Orville?"

"Not yet. We're working on it. I'll pass on what I can when we get something."

The chairman left as the D.A. was placing a call to a friend of his in the army personnel section in Washington. The officer was out so he left a message to return his call. His secretary buzzed his intercom, telling him he had a call from Colorado Springs.

"This is Sergeant Don Stone. My partner and I are in the Springs. The locals up here picked up one Eldon Jones driving the late sheriff's Cadillac. We spent half the night talking with the kid and got nothing.

We ran his name and found out he has three priors, burglary, possession of drugs with intent and assault. All charges filed by the sheriff's department. We would like to hang onto him, bring him back down there and work him for a possible on the sheriff," Stone told him.

"Can you make a case for the car theft starting here?" the D.A. asked.

"He boosted it from the motel parking lot. That he did admit." Stone said.

"I'll get a warrant on the car theft, fax a copy up there. You should be on your way back shortly," the D.A. said then hung up the phone.

Jerry Magee was at his desk by seven. He found out from dispatch that Stone and Rehaus were still up in Colorado Springs. He worked files on other open cases and by ten was getting hungry. All he had for breakfast was coffee and a roll. He went out to his car and drove to a restaurant where he ordered a big breakfast. The waitress brought his order and he started eating when the chief deputy of Pueblo County slid into the booth across from him. He had never met the chief but was aware of her. No one had figured why the sheriff had appointed a woman to be his chief deputy unless it was for her looks. She was beautiful. Her skin was dark as though tanned, but he was sure it was from her ethnic background. Short black hair, large eyes, full mouth and really built. He guessed her to be somewhere in her mid thirties. The first thing his eyes checked out was her chest, then her wedding ring finger. Chest great. No ring on the finger. Her uniform fit her very well. It was immaculate. Sharp creases, leather polished to a bright sheen.

"I'm Penny Booker, sergeant. I don't think we have ever met," she said. Nice voice, he thought.

"A pleasure to meet you deputy," he responded taking her offered hand and shaking it. Nice soft skin, he thought again.

"Do you know the county board chairman, Elmer Gray?" she asked.

"You want some coffee or something?" he asked.

"No thanks. You know him?"

"Never met him, why?"

"He came in my office this morning and said the board was considering you for Orville Boone's vacated position. I was supposed to check you out."

"This is news to me. Why would he or the board be considering me for county sheriff?"

"He says the idea was Walt Sugdens."

"Good old Walt. He must figure I don't have enough to do. Why aren't you in line for the job?"

"Don't want it!"

"Why not?"

"I have enough headaches with the job I have, without asking for more."

"Would you kick my ass if I told you something?"

"What?"

"You are stunning. No, you are beautiful!" He could swear this caused her to blush.

"I could you know!"

"Could what?"

"Kick your ass if I was a mind to! You meant it didn't you."

"Yes. I'm surprised you don't hear it all the time."

"You meant it without an ulterior motive."

"What would that ulterior motive be?"

"Like trying to get into my pants!"

"I wouldn't try that, especially if you could kick my ass. I don't buy your reason for not going after the sheriff's job."

"It took me two years to prove myself in the job I got. It would take forever to get accepted as the sheriff. The hard part would be at the next election."

"I can understand that. You're not very subtle about checking me out."

"I figured, why waste time. Go right to the man himself."

"How did you find me?"

"Your dispatcher. We have your radio frequency. You checked out here for something to eat. The hash browns look delicious."

Magee handed her his salad fork. She took it and scooped up some potatoes from his plate.

"I love potatoes but too many and I get fat."

"You don't have an ounce of fat anywhere."

"That you can see. If you considered the sheriff's job, you think you can straighten the place out?"

"Why? Does it need straightening out?"

"Orville Boone was a piss poor sheriff. There are many things that need fixed."

"You know how to do it?"

"I can tell you what needs fixed. It will take someone like you to fix it."

"I'm not going to eat the rest of that bacon."

"Thanks," she said, picking it up and shoving it in her mouth. "I have to go. If you consider the offer, I will help. See you around."

She slid out of the booth and walked away. Magee felt warm all over just watching her behind as she left.

He finished eating, lit a cigarette and sat drinking his coffee. The short talk with Penny Booker had stirred his need for female companionship. He had been so busy since coming to Pueblo, finding a woman had been hidden at the back of his mind somewhere. Must be getting old when I'm too busy to get horny, he thought. Penny Booker was certainly someone to fire up his furnace again. He ran what little information he had about the late sheriff's homicide through his mind. What to do next? He left the booth, paid for the meal and returned to his car. He drove across the city to the run down commercial district, parked on the street in front of a small store building with Dykes Pawn Shop stenciled across the large front window. He went inside and spotted Virgil Dykes sitting on a stool behind the well-worn counter.

"Let me guess. You pulled the Boone murder case and came to old Virgil for information," the man said.

"You have it figured right, Virgil. I thought if anyone in this entire state would know about the late Sheriff Orville Boone, it would be you," Magee responded.

"There are probably two or three dozen people out there who will be happy to hear the old fart is dead," Dykes said.

"You and I have had several conversations about the criminal element in this city. How come you never said anything about the sheriff?"

"You never asked?"

"I'm asking now!"

"Orville Boone was smart about some things and dumber than a post about others. He was into everything that came his way, payoffs from roadhouses with a little gambling in the back, shakedowns on illegals coming up here to work. He made all the working girls kick in a part of their hard earned pay to keep from going to jail. He sampled a few himself, free of charge, of course. He protected a few of the boys who boosted cars, and chopped them down for parts. He stayed clear of the big boys but he sure controlled all the small operations," Dykes said.

"How did he get away with it so long?"

"Like I said. He kept it small. A little help here, a little there, plain and simple. He allowed two or three of his deputies in on the action. They handled any heavy work. The sheriff didn't dirty his hands personally."

"He lived pretty well. What kept everyone off his back? They had to know he was spending a hell of a lot more than his salary?"

"Everyone knows his wife has big money. I figure that's why he stayed with her. Let them think she was paying."

"Why did she put up with it?"

"Don't know. You'll have to ask her."

"Stone and Rehaus picked up one Eldon Jones driving the late sheriff's Cadillac. Would he have any reason to kill Boone?"

"Small time doper. He would boost a few cars for the chop shops, anything to get a few bucks to buy dope. He wouldn't know what to do with a gun. Not your man. Look for someone close to Boone. Someone he screwed over, maybe one of the hookers, maybe his wife!"

"Thanks for the info, I owe you one," Magee said, starting for the door.

"I hear they want you to be the new sheriff. You gonna do it?"

"Word travels fast around here. I won't ask how you know this. What do you think?"

"Would be a hell of an improvement," Dykes said.

Magee went to the car and drove back to police headquarters. He glanced at his watch as he pulled the chair back from his desk. It was past noon but he wouldn't be hungry until suppertime. He looked out into the squad room as Stone and Rehaus came through with a prisoner. A young, emaciated looking black man, his hands cuffed behind his back, was being pushed ahead of Stone toward the detention cell in the back. Magee walked out into the large room and toward the desk where both detectives worked. Stone slammed the door on the cell, then came back and sat down at his desk.

"Well, we solved this one for you," Stone said, a smug look on his face.

"You're making that kid the shooter?" Magee asked.

"Sure as hell. He's guilty as sin," Stone responded.

"How so?"

"He stole the car. He said he took it around midnight. The coroner puts the time of death about then. He has a long rap sheet. All the arrests made by the sheriff's office. He had Boone's wallet on him and he was seen in the motel around 11:00 Saturday night," Stone said, enunciating each word.

"Did you find the gun?"

"No!"

"What's his motive?"

"He hated the sheriff for putting him behind bars where he couldn't get at his dope," Stone responded as though this point should be evident.

Magee walked back to the holding cell. Jones was lying on the hard bunk, his eyes closed. His left eye was puffy and his lip was split. He opened his eyes when he heard Magee approach.

"When was the last time you shot up Eldon?" Magee asked.

"I ain't on that stuff no more."

"You know that's bull Eldon. When you have been locked up a few hours, you will not be able to hide your condition. Those detectives tell me you killed Sheriff Orville Boone."

"They're lying then. I ain't killed nobody."

"Did you steal the sheriff's car?"

"I took the Caddy. I didn't even know it was the sheriff's until I went through the billfold."

"Where did you get the billfold?"

"It was lying on the seat when I got in. I was clear up in the springs and it was day time before I saw it."

"How did you get the cut on your lip and the swelling around your eye?"

"That fat cop knocked me around, trying to make me say I killed the sheriff."

"Did you know the sheriff?"

"I knew him. He never knocked me around. Had his deputies do it while he watched."

"What were you doing in the motel Saturday night?"

"I was looking for a friend."

"Who?"

"Dixie Flagg."

"I know Dixie. You were trying to score some dope from her. Did you find her?"

"No. It was raining. I figured she was downtown somewhere."

"Where were you going to take the car Eldon, to a chop shop?"

"I don't know nothin about a chop shop."

"You take it easy Eldon. We'll talk again later," Magee said as he walked away from the cell. He walked past Stone and Rehaus and went into his office. He sat down behind the desk as the phone rang.

"Can you come back here a minute?" Lieutenant Winters said.

"Be right there," Magee said. He went back out and down the hallway to the lieutenant's office and found Winters on the phone. He waived Magee in and pointed at a chair. Magee sat down and lit a cigarette. Winters finished his phone conversation and hung up.

"Stone and Rehaus have it all wrapped up. Good work. I figured it would take longer than this. Those two did most of the legwork and picked up the guy. Let them finish it. You can get back to your regular files," the lieutenant said.

"The black kid didn't do it!" Magee said.

"What?"

"He didn't do it."

"Well the D.A. must think we have enough on the kid. He told Stone to book him on murder one."

"The D.A. will need more than Stone has to get a conviction."

"Let it go Magee. Move on to other things. Now get on with it," the lieutenant said in dismissal.

Magee went downstairs and out of the building. The afternoon sky was overcast, a cold wind blowing off the mountains. He backed the car out and left the lot. He drove across the city to a seedy bar on the west side. He parked across the street and walked down the alley and through the back door of the place. The bartender stood behind the counter watching some talk show on the small television hanging from the wall. Magee stopped just inside, waiting for his eyes to adjust to the dim light. He saw one man on a stool at the bar, another at a table by the front door and thought his luck was good as he spotted who he was looking for. She was sitting in a booth near the front.

He walked down through the tables and slid into the booth across from her.

"Hello Dixie. You're up early today," he said in greeting.

"Sergeant Jerico Magee. I figured to see you before this," Dixie replied.

Magee paused, looking at her. Dixie Flagg had been cute when she was younger. He would guess she was somewhere around forty now, a little heavy around the waist. Too much eye make up yet still attractive enough to lure her customers. She began selling her favors before she was sixteen. It was all she knew how to do. The first thing he did when he started working as a homicide detective, was find some snitches. He needed street people as a source of information. Virgil Dykes had been first. Dixie Flagg had been the next one he groomed as a source. He had been civil to both of them and tried to treat them with some measure of compassion for the lives they led.

"I take that to mean you expected me to come asking about the late sheriff," Magee said.

"My you are perceptive."

"There is no need to be snotty Dixie. Tell me what you know about Orville Boone."

"You'll have to look a long time to find anyone sorry he's dead."

"That includes you?"

"Especially me."

"You ever sleep with him?"

"More than I care to say."

"Blackmail?"

"You could call it that. I either slept with him or went to jail."

"He was working his strong arm right here in the city?"

"In the city, out in the county. It didn't make any difference to him."

"You had to kick back some of your take?"

"A hundred a week. Every week. Just like clockwork."

"You handed the money to him?"

"Oh no, not in person. Joe Black was who I paid."

"Who is Joe Black?"

"One of his deputies. He had three doing all the dirty work. Black, Everett Cline and Glenn Dunn."

"Did you ever tell anyone about the shakedown?"

"Tell who. Oh yea, I did tell someone once. I bailed out a friend of mine once when a state cop picked her up. I told the guy we paid enough protection that we shouldn't be hassled. Word got back to Boone and Black paid me a visit. My face wasn't pretty for two weeks. I never told anyone again."

"Any word about what other enterprises he was into?"

"The most talk was about a big chop shop set up."

"Where?"

"Somewhere in the county. It's supposed to be big. Stolen cars come in from three or four states."

"Anything else?"

"Gambling, green card protection, tax free cigarettes, you name it, he was in the middle of it."

"How about drugs?"

"The word was he stayed clear of anything big. He would squeeze users but never went near dealers."

"There's a black kid by the name of Eldon Jones that's sitting in jail accused of shooting him. He do it?"

"I'd be damned surprised. Where would he get a gun? Every dime he gets goes into his arm."

"He was caught driving the sheriff's car."

"He occasionally boosts cars on his own. Sells them for dope money."

"If you hear anything about a name for the sheriff's shooter, I would appreciate a call," Magee told her.

"You going to take the job?"

"What job?"

"Being county sheriff!"

"Where did you hear that?"

"It's all over the street. Most people I know say you would be a good sheriff."

"No one has approached me about being sheriff."

"They will. If you take over, could you look into something for me?"

"Sure. I owe you. What is it?"

"Word is, there are about a dozen young girls that were hauled up here from Mexico with the promise of good jobs. They were set up in a house and are forced to service the migrant workers at twenty to forty dollars a trick. They get to keep two or three. The rest goes to pay off transportation costs. Some of them are only fourteen."

"Where's the house and who is doing this?"

"Don't know on either question. I just hear bits and pieces of this. Can you do anything?"

"I can try. Thanks for the help. You need any money?"

"I always need money but I ain't chargen you for this. I wouldn't charge you for anything else either," she said, smiling at him.

"Stay out of jail Dixie," he said then stood up and left. She watched him as he walked away, thinking how things might have been if she had never come to this God forsaken town. Sergeant Jerico Magee was one good-looking dude. She felt a calm peace when she was around him. She thought he could be deadly though, if provoked far enough.

Magee was back in his office at three. He found a message to call the D.A. He picked up the phone and dialed the number from memory.

"District Attorney's Office," his secretary responded on the phone.

"This is Jerry Magee, is the D.A. in?"

"He's expecting your call, Sergeant Magee. One moment please," she responded.

"Can you meet me for supper?" the D.A. asked when he came on the line.

"Where and when?" Magee responded.

"Seven at Sammy Chen's!"

"See you then," Magee responded and hung up. He worked on the files on his desk until five thirty then drove home. He shaved, took a bath and picked out some clean clothes. At six thirty he drove downtown to a steak house owned and operated by Sammy Chen and his wife. He and Sugden had eaten there several times. Long enough for Chen to call them by their first names. The hostess led him to a table and he ordered a beer. He lit a cigarette and looked around at the people eating. The restaurant served good food and the prices were not cheap. He was about to order another beer when the D.A. came through the door. A well-dressed man who was probably in his late fifties accompanied him. He looked like a politician.

"Jerry, let me introduce Elmer Gray. Elmer is the chairman of the Pueblo County Board of Commissioners. Elmer, this is Jerry Magee," the D.A. said.

Magee stood up to shake hands with the chairman, and then they both found a chair on each side of him. He felt like he was being surrounded. A waiter appeared to see what they were drinking.

"I apologize for not talking to you earlier, but it has been a busy day. Elmer wanted to meet with you and I thought this would be a good time."

"With the death of Orville Boone, we have two choices to fill the vacancy. We can have a special election now or appoint someone for the remaining two years. Walter says you are the man for the job. Would you consider it?" Gray said.

"You two don't mess around, but get right to it. Why not go for a special election?" Magee responded.

"It's not political consideration, as you might think," Gray responded. "Or in one sense, maybe it is. If we held a special election, chances are three to one a politician will win when we need a professional right now. A good professional would have a head start of two years to clean up the department before they would have to run for the office. A simple reply is that we need a professional right now to clean house."

"I don't have to ask how much you have to do with this old buddy," Magee said to the D.A. "What would I have to work with?"

"There are currently thirty five working for the sheriff. Authorized sworn positions are forty but Orville always kept about ten positions vacant. I have no idea why. You are aware that the bulk of the population is right here in Pueblo. That makes most of the everyday problems Chief Morrison's headaches. The primary function of the department is court work, transporting prisoners, patrolling the county and enforcing the law outside of the city. I would hope a new sheriff could establish a working relationship with the city and the state that does not now exist," the chairman said.

"What about money?"

"The budget has never been a problem. We appropriate more than Orville ever spent. Salaries are equal to or a little better than other places. Most of the people are members of the union and are also subject to state civil service rules."

"I had a visit from Chief Deputy Booker. Tell me about her," Magee said.

"Very competent. She could run the department but she couldn't carry enough muscle to clean house."

"I figure you want an answer yesterday," Magee said. "Give me time to have another talk with Booker. I'll let you know in the morning,"

"Fair enough sergeant," Gray responded. "Let's eat, I'm starved."

They ordered supper and made small talk until the food came. Gray talked about county government. He spoke from twenty years experience. Magee thought him to be a reasonable individual with common sense. He finished eating and excused himself telling them he had another meeting before he got to go home for the evening. When he was alone with Magee, the D.A. talked about himself.

"Gray was responsible for me being D.A. here. I came here as an assistant and my boss retired mid term. He is an honest commissioner who really wants to do it right. Not too many like him around."

"How long have you been here?" Magee asked him.

"Just a little over a year. Look, I have a selfish motive pushing you for the job. I picked up enough in my short time as D.A. to know that Boone was dirty. Who was I going to get to go after him? I briefly discussed it with your Chief Morrison and he ignored me. Treated me like a younger brother who wanted to borrow his fifty-seven Chevy. I thought about going to the attorney general and asking for state help but haven't done it. When you came along, I felt like someone turned on a light in the dark closet. I checked you out pretty thorough. I have a college friend who ended up in army personnel. You have some military record," Sugden told him.

"I said I would consider it. Finish up your desert. I want to get out of here before you start singing the star spangled banner," Magee said.

Sugden smiled at him and finished his supper. They walked out together with Magee promising to call him the next day.

Magee climbed into his car and called dispatch on his cellular phone. He asked for Penny Booker's home address and wrote it in his pocket notebook. He was surprised that she lived in a nice ranch style house. He drove to the house and parked on the street in front. He left the car, walked across the front lawn and knocked at her door.

"I took a chance you might be off duty. I apologize for coming to your home but I need to talk," he said to her when she opened the door. She stood looking at him a moment then opened the door. He went in and waited as she closed the door.

"This is the first night I've been home for a week. Come in," she responded leading him down a short hall into her living room. She went to the television and turned it off.

"You had supper?" she asked.

"I ate with Walter Sugden and Elmer Gray," he responded. He was distracted by what she was wearing. She had on sweat pants and a matching sweatshirt. They fit her very well. He was confident she wasn't wearing a bra.

"They made you the offer! What did you say?"

"I told them it would depend on talking with you before I decided."

"Then I guess that should make me nervous but it doesn't. I'm selfish enough to say what I want. Why did you tell them you wanted my input?"

"It sounds like you are the one that makes the place run. I need you on my side to make the wheels turn. Can you work with me?"

"My gut instinct tells me yes, unless you have a dark side. Is there something in your nature I should look out for?"

"Just my distraction?"

"Your distraction. What's that?"

"Working around someone as good looking as you. Is there someone special in your life?"

"Now I would normally say that is none of your business, but I doubt if you and I will have a normal relationship. You're not put off that I'm a woman in this position."

"No more than you will be put off that I'm a man. I got past that years ago in the army. We both know we will have to respect each other's abilities. All I can do is keep the relationship in perspective and businesslike. The distraction I will have to get used to is being around a well built, pleasant, good-looking woman. I never had to do that before."

"You never worked with women before?"

"None as attractive as you!"

"I'm already finding out you have a line of bull shit!"

"Boone had three deputies doing the heavy work. Everett Cline, Joe Black and Glenn Dunn. They would be our first order of business."

"Sounds like you have been digging. You're right about those three. They need to go."

"They need to go to jail. What about the rest of the deputies?"

"We have some good people, if they were turned loose so they could do their jobs."

Chapter 3

8:00 a.m. Tuesday
Jan. 4, 2000

Magee talked with Chief Deputy Penny Booker until almost midnight on Monday, then drove home to get some sleep. He was in his office at police headquarters before eight, sitting at his desk drinking coffee and contemplating what to do about the job change. His instincts told him to let it pass. He was settled in at his present job. If he took on the sheriff's job, there would be months of nothing but problems, confrontations and headaches. One thing in favor of taking on the job was his feeling that things would soon start going to hell where he was.

Lieutenant Aaron Winters had embraced Sergeant Stone's choice as the sheriff's killer and had already wrapped the case up in his mind. It was too quick. Anyone that paid any attention to what Stone did or said was either as dumb as he was or didn't give a damn. He thought that was enough of a warning of things to come. He picked up the phone and dialed Elmer Gray's number. He told Gray he would take the job. Gray asked about when he would start. He told him it would be up to how his boss took the news. Gray said he would have the board vote on him at their meeting this morning. When he got off the phone with Gray, he dialed the D.A.'s number.

"I told Gray I would do it," he said when Sugden answered.

"Great. When do you start?" the D.A. responded.

"Don't know yet. I'll tell Sugden and see what he says. "What about Eldon Jones. Sugden says you think you have enough to charge him."

"Jones is scheduled for a preliminary hearing at 11:00 this morning. You don't sound like you're happy about that."

"He didn't do it!"

"What? Why do you say that?"

"He says he didn't do it!"

"Aw for Christ's sake Jerry, they all say that. He was at the motel. He took the sheriff's car. He had the sheriff's wallet. He was a three time looser, all at the hands of the sheriff. It's enough to get him nailed at a preliminary," the D.A. said.

"No gun. The motive is too thin. There is a long list of suspects out there with a much better motive."

"One other thing you probably don't know. They came up with a witness who says Jones threatened to kill the sheriff."

"Who came up with that?"

"Stone and Rehaus. The last time Jones was in the county jail, the guy in the cell with him said he threatened to shoot the sheriff. Said he was getting tired of being knocked around by the sheriff and his pigs," the D.A. said. "We have plenty of time to come up with the gun and more evidence before it goes to trial."

"Your call, old buddy. I still say you're wasting your time, now about this new job. The first order of business will be the dirty deputies. I'll gather up what I can and put it on your desk and go from there," Magee said.

"Get settled in first. Keep in touch," the D.A. said, and then hung up.

Magee put the phone down, lit a cigarette and leaned back in his chair. He sat thinking about his conversation with Sugden. He left the office and walked back to Lieutenant Winters' office. He knocked on the open door and Winters waived him in.

"You're going to take the job!" Winters said. It was more of a statement than a question.

"It's amazing how news travels around this town so fast. Yea, I thought I'd give it a shot," Magee said.

"Well, I'm sorry to lose you, but I also know they need a good man over there. I guess I can give you up for such a good cause. When do you want to go?" the lieutenant asked.

"I told them it was up to when you would turn me loose."

"Well, it's not as though we didn't have anyone to do the work. I would prefer a couple weeks, but I think you could do more good spending the two weeks over there. Tell them you're free at the end of the day. Turn you're active files over to the steno pool and brief Stone and Rehaus on anything they need to know. I'll notify personnel and the chief. I do this with the intent to improve relations with the sheriff's department. Knowing we can work with you will be an asset for both departments. You have done a good job for us Magee, I'm looking forward to working with you as sheriff," the lieutenant said as he stood up and shook hands with Magee. Knowing this was his dismissal; he thanked the lieutenant and left his office. He returned to his desk and piled his active case folders on the desk. He gathered up the few personal possessions he kept in the office. He went to the personnel office, turned in his files and visited with the secretary. He went back to the lieutenant's office and found out Winters was gone. He turned in his shield and gun to Winters' secretary. He went downstairs to the front desk and handed the duty sergeant, Patrick Lopez the keys to his city car.

"It is a sad day that you are leaving us Jerico Magee," the sergeant said.

"It is amazing how fast you hear everything Lopez. It has been a pleasure working with you," Magee told him.

"Now don't be a stranger around here. We will look forward to seeing your smiling face very soon," Lopez said.

"Can you find me a ride to my house?" Magee asked.

"You go out in front and I'll have dispatch send a car along to take you there," the sergeant told him. Magee left through the front door and climbed in the front seat of the cruiser officer James Red Bear was driving.

"I thought you were off until Wednesday?" Magee said as he got in the car.

"They were short on this shift as usual and I got called in. I hear you are about to be the new sheriff," Red Bear said.

"I guess I will be soon. I'll miss working with you," he responded.

"Now we can see if you mean that, should you get over there and find you have an opening. I wouldn't mind being a deputy sheriff," Red Bear said.

"You're serious?" Magee asked.

"Sure am. With the wide-open spaces the deputies have to patrol, I figure there are times when horses will be used. Always wanted to ride a horse!"

"You never rode a horse?"

"I'm from California. My mom and dad are both professors at UCLA. I'm an urban Indian."

"How did you get way out here?"

"I was stationed out here in the air force. I just stayed after I got out."

"I'll see what I have to work with and will keep in touch," he said. Red Bear pulled the cruiser into the curb in front of his house and stopped. Magee struggled with the small box carrying his personal possessions, and left the car. He thanked Red Bear and went inside as the car drove off.

The phone was ringing as he unlocked the door. He put the box down and picked up the phone.

"The board vote was unanimous to appoint you sheriff," Elmer Gray said. "I called the station and they said you were already gone. If you can come down to the courthouse after lunch, I have the judge lined up to swear you in."

"I just as well get started," Magee responded. "See you then." He put the phone down and went to the bedroom. He picked out a good sports jacket and slacks. He found a clean dress shirt and tie, and then took everything to the bathroom to change.

When he was ready, he went out in back of the house to a small one-car garage where he kept his personal vehicle. It was a ninety-two Jeep Cherokee, which he hadn't started for weeks. He was pleasantly surprised when it started right off. He drove across town to the courthouse and was in the judge's chambers at 1:00 p.m.

Elmer Gray, two of the commissioners and Chief Deputy Penny Booker, joined him. The judge administered his oath of office then Elmer handed him his shield. Penny told him they had a supply of weapons at the office. He could pick what he wanted. Before he left, he asked the judge about the preliminary hearing for Eldon Jones. He said that Jones was bound over on a murder one charge. Magee asked if he had an attorney. The Judge said he had no money and a public defender was appointed to represent him. He said the attorney up on the list was one Margaret Patterson. He thanked the judge for the information, and then thanked the commissioners for their confidence in him.

He followed Penny out of the courthouse, picked up his Jeep and followed her cruiser to the sheriff's office. He was surprised to find that it was a modern one-story building covering half a city block. He parked in back beside Penny and followed her in the back door. They came into a large room with several desks. Uniformed deputies sat at three desks. They turned to watch him as he came in. Penny took him to his office at the far end of the building. She showed him her office, the interrogation rooms, the front desk, the dispatcher's office, a meeting room, coffee room and six cells on the other side of the building. She ended up the tour back at his office. A woman sat at a desk in the squad room, just outside his door. She introduced him to Emma White, his new secretary. Emma was a woman in her early sixties. She had aged very well and could pass for much younger. She was well dressed, her gray hair cut short and she smiled at Magee when she was introduced.

"Emma has been here for a long time," Penny said. "You will soon find out she can make things so much easier around here."

"It is very nice to meet you Emma," Magee said.

"Welcome Sheriff Magee. Don't listen to Penny, I just do what I'm told," she said.

"Give me a little time with him Emma, then he's all yours," Penny said.

She followed Magee into the office and pulled a chair up to the front of his desk as he went around behind and sat down. Magee looked around the office. It was sparsely decorated. He pulled open the desk drawers, finding very little in them.

"Let's start off with our people. What positions of rank are there?"

"Just the sheriff and chief deputy. Everyone else is a deputy, dispatcher or secretary," Penny responded.

"The dispatcher's are deputies?"

"Yes."

"No detectives?"

"None!"

"Well, lets start with organizing the personnel. What is our work load?"

"Maybe we better ask Emma in now," she said. She went to the door and spoke to Emma. She came in carrying a file, which she handed to Magee, then pulled a chair up to the desk for herself. He opened a steno book and waited as he read through the file.

"Well it's evident that Boone played his cards pretty close to his chest. Let's start off with the dispatchers. Penny, figure out how many you need to operate twenty-four hours. Hire some people. All the dispatchers will be civilians. Make one of them supervisor of the department. Pick out four deputies for detectives to do most of the investigations. Three of them will be sergeants; one will be a lieutenant in charge, the same with the patrol section with a lieutenant in charge. Try to find us at least six more deputies. Start with Officer Red Bear, he would be a good candidate for the head of the patrol section. Now I know you have to work with the civil service rules, but you can make it happen. Be prepared to replace as many as four deputies that may not like my changes. Find me some uniforms and work me into a shift. Set up a duty officer responsible for each shift. Keep me free of that job. What about vehicles?" Magee said.

"We have twelve cruisers, two four wheel drive utility vehicles and four saddle horses," Penny responded.

"We do have horses!" he exclaimed. "Where do you keep them?"

"At the county ranch," she said.

"County ranch?"

"It was originally a place for the homeless to live. There isn't a lot left there now. It's more like an acreage than a ranch."

"You may have to buy more cruisers. We'll wait until you get new schedules worked out before we know. Emma, work me up a schedule on salaries and what other counties this size pay. Keep it plain and simple. That's another point. Spread the word to everyone about paper work. I'm not interested in long, boring reports. Keep everything plain and simple. We work toward eliminating all the paper work not absolutely essential. We want good information for the D. A.'s office, nothing more. We'll wait until Monday to have a meeting with all the people. By then, you may have the new plan ready to show them. This should keep Emma busy for a while. Now, will you take me to supply, I want to pick out a weapon. Then let's look at the vehicles and you can take me out to this county ranch," he told Penny. Emma left the office without a word.

"What will be her reaction?" he asked Penny.

"It will be positive. She has been well aware of the changes that are long overdue. I forgot the store room and evidence rooms on the tour," she said.

Magee followed her out of the office and to the storeroom. Inside the room was an evidence vault. She showed him the arsenal of weapons. He picked out a 9mm Ruger with a belt holster and a shoulder holster. She told him all the cruisers had a shotgun in a rack up front and extra ammo in the trunk. He picked up extra clips for the gun and told her to check it out to him. He clipped the belt holster on, inserted a full clip and inserted the gun in the holster. She took him out to the parking lot and showed him the car the sheriff drove. It was an expensive Chrysler with no markings.

"I don't think I'll drive this. Trade it in on something cheaper. I'll drive something with no markings but I'll need a radio, a cellular phone, a hidden siren and red lights. Let's take your car," he said. He got in the passenger seat and Penny drove out of the parking lot. She said the ranch was not far from where Boone's widow lives.

"Do you have any files on the three deputies in question?" he asked.

"Nothing. I figured they would find anything left at the office," she replied.

"Start working up files on all three. Take them home with you. Between the two of us, we'll build a case on them," he said.

The county ranch was twenty acres of pastureland. There was a large ranch house, that was home in years past, for a number of residents with no home of their own. A large barn, a corral and two smaller buildings sat back from the house. Penny took him to the corral to see the horses. The caretaker who came out of the barn to see who was there joined them.

"Sheriff, this is Charley Little Crow. He lives in the house and takes care of the place. He is the only one not considered a deputy. He's been out here for a number of years. Charley, this is the new sheriff, Jerico Magee," Penny said.

Magee shook hands with him. He couldn't have been much older than Magee. He wore faded blue jeans, a western shirt and hat and a worn pair of western boots.

"Do you know Jimmy Red Bear?" Magee asked him.

"Heard about him. He's a city cop," Little Crow responded.

"He expressed a desire to ride your horses. They look like good stock," Magee said. Little Crow didn't have much to say. Penny broke the silence by taking Magee to the house and showing him around, and then they left and started back to the city.

"He's a man of few words," Magee said when they were in the car.

"He's dependable. Takes good care of the ranch. Emma speaks kindly of him. That is a good recommendation," Penny said.

They returned to the sheriff's building a little before 5:00. He left Penny and went to his office.

"There is a lady waiting to see you sheriff," his secretary said as he went through the door.

She was sitting in the only comfortable chair in the office. Looking back, Magee remembered meeting Margaret Patterson, and how his first sight of her caused a sensation in his stomach like none he ever felt before. She was dressed in a tight fitting blue skirt, a soft pink blouse, a beige suit jacket and her hair was put up on her head. She was probably in her mid thirties he thought. Her blouse was nicely filled out. She had the prettiest green eyes. He had never seen anyone with such green eyes. Her nose was a little too wide but her mouth compensated for it, balancing out the whole face. He first saw her profile. She was lovely. She was also smoking a cigarette. She crushed the cigarette out in an ashtray as he came in and stood up, forgetting a briefcase on her lap, which crashed to the floor, spilling papers all over. He stopped midway to his desk and bent down to help her. His head struck hers, knocking her backwards, sprawling onto the floor. Her skirt rode up above her knees, exposing the smooth skin on her thighs and the blue silk material of her panties.

"Shit!" He said, grabbing her arm, trying to help her up. "I'm sorry."

She struggled to get her feet under her, trying to stand up. She grabbed his arm for help and he was off balance enough, that she pulled him down on the floor with her. He landed, sprawled across her, pinning her to the floor. He was so shocked; he just lay there a moment. When he finally struggled up off her, he twisted around, sitting on the floor beside her. He looked up and saw his secretary Emma, standing in the doorway looking at them. The situation was so bizarre, two grown people lying on the floor he started to laugh. At first Patterson was furious until she caught his mood and started to laugh with him. Her hair came loose when she fought to get back up. It fell down to her shoulders and across her face. One eye was covered. When their laughter diminished, he spoke to her.

"Now if you will just stay like that for a moment, I'm going to get up," he said. He stood up and offered his hand. She took it and he helped her to her feet. He than leaned over, gathering up her papers and briefcase and put them on his desk. He pulled her chair up in front of the desk, then went around behind and sat down. She was busy stuffing the papers back in her briefcase.

He looked at Emma who just rolled her eyes and went back to her desk.

"I'm sorry about the collision. Does your head hurt?" He said.

"I'll be fine," she responded, rubbing the spot where his head hit her.

"I'm Jerry Magee, how can I help you," he said standing up to offer her his hand. She reached across the desk, shook his hand then sat back down.

"You can start by not yelling at me when I light a cigarette. I need one," she responded. She looked around for her purse and spotted it lying on the floor behind her. She got up, put it on the desk, rummaged around inside and came up with a package of cigarettes and a lighter. Her hand shook as she put the cigarette in her mouth. Magee was standing beside her now and held out his lighter for her. She told him thank you and he went back and sat down. He lit a cigarette and pushed an ashtray across the desk for her to use.

"There are so damn many people around who think it is their duty to treat smokers like second class citizens, I guess I'm defensive about it. I'm Margaret Patterson. I'm a practicing attorney who has been appointed to defend Eldon Jones," she told him.

Her jacket was open in front and hung down beside each breast. Her nipples were hard and projected through the material of her blouse. He tried not to stare but was losing the battle.

"How did you get stuck with that job?" he asked.

"The judge just told me it was my turn. He has a list of attorneys and no one argues with him, at least not any of the attorneys new to practice in his jurisdiction. I came here to find out why Jones was charged with murder on such little evidence," she responded.

"Why me. It's not my case. Besides, I don't work for the Pueblo police department any more," he said.

"They told me the case was assigned to you."

"Well they didn't tell you the whole story. The case was mine at first, then the chief of detectives gave it to one Sergeant Donald Stone."

"Well, whoever is in charge, doesn't know what the hell he is doing. I was surprised the judge ruled for the D.A.'s office to charge Jones."

"So was I!"

"What?"

"I was just as surprised as you. Jones didn't kill Orville Boone."

"Then why did the D.A. file on him?"

"You will have to ask the D.A. that."

"Well then I guess I'm wasting your time," she said standing to leave.

"How long have you been practicing law?"

"Six months. I'm working with Arthur Nash. He's been in business here for many years," she responded. "I apologize sheriff. I can see I need to go see the district attorney."

"How's your head?" he said, trying to prolong the meeting.

"Well I guess there is a slight swelling," she said, rubbing her head.

He walked around the desk, put his hand on her head, parted the hair and looked. "You're right, there's a pretty good bump there."

She surprised him and did the same, putting her fingers on his head, feeling through his close-cropped hair.

"You have one about the same size," she responded. He picked up that she was in no hurry to leave. Penny Booker came in the door then and interrupted their mutual head feeling.

"Excuse me boss, I didn't know you were with someone," Booker said.

"Penny, this is Margaret Patterson. She's been appointed to represent the man accused of killing Orville Boone. Miss Patterson, this is Chief Deputy Penny Booker."

"Maddie. Everyone calls me Maddie," the young attorney said shaking Penny's hand.

"I've seen you in the courthouse before Maddie. You new to the city?" Penny asked.

"Six months. I guess you could say I'm new. This is my first case in court," Maddie responded.

"Your first here or your first ever?" Magee asked.

"My first ever. I tried to tell the judge that but he wouldn't listen. I'm a bit nervous about the case but I know enough about the law to know they don't have proof that Eldon Jones killed the late sheriff," she said.

"Deputy Booker and I are working late tonight. We were just about to go out for some supper, would you care to join us?" Magee asked her.

Penny looked at Magee with her eyes wide and the expression of this is the first I heard of an invite for supper.

"If you don't mind. I came here in a cab. I would appreciate a lift and I do have to eat," Maddie said.

"Great," Magee said. "Let's all go then." He led them out of the building and to his Jeep in the parking lot. He opened the door for Maddie to sit in the front seat. Penny got in the back saying to herself just an hour ago I got all the attention.

Penny directed him to a family restaurant and they were soon seated at a table, looking through the menu.

"Are you a native of Colorado?" Penny asked Maddie.

"I'm originally from Madison, Wisconsin. My folks live in Denver now. I went to school at the University of Nebraska out at Lincoln. Arthur Nash is a good friend of my father. When I passed the bar exam, he suggested I come down and work with him for a while to gain some experience. I found a nice apartment and moved down last fall," Maddie said.

Maddie and Penny talked about their lives all through the meal. They seemed to establish a friendship. They both ignored Magee, which didn't bother him at all. He just ate, watching both of them, feeling good to be in the presence of two very beautiful women.

"My car pooped out on me last week and has been in the shop. It's a pain to get around in cabs," Maddie was telling Penny.

"Well if you get in a bind getting somewhere, give me a call. I'll come pick you up and give you a ride," Penny said.

By the time the meal was finished, they had arranged to get together later in the week for lunch. Magee paid for the meal and they went out to his Jeep. Maddie directed him to her apartment house where they dropped her off at the curb. Penny transferred to the front seat, waiving at Maddie as she went up the walk to the entrance to her building.

"You can put your eyeballs back in and pull up your bottom lip," Penny said as he drove off.

"Am I that obvious," he responded.

"If you were superman, that poor girl would have X-ray burns all over her boobs," Penny said.

"She is very good looking," he said.

"She seems very nice too. She may be in over her head defending Jones. I wonder why a judge would give her the job," she said.

"We are discreetly going to continue an investigation into Boone's death. Something is definitely wrong. A blind man could see that Eldon Jones didn't kill him. Someone wants him to take the fall for it though. I hope you didn't have something planned. I wanted to go through some personnel files with you. We should be out of there in a couple hours," Magee said.

It was after midnight, when he noticed the time. They had reviewed the file of everyone on the payroll. The files of Everett Cline, Joe Black and Glenn Dunn were lying on his desk. Cline and Black started about the time Boone was first elected. Dunn joined them three years later. Nothing in the files would help them with their investigation. Magee saw Penny yawning. He told her to put the files back and they would call it a night. He turned the light off and was about to leave the office behind her when the phone rang. The dispatcher told him it was a Margaret Patterson asking for him.

"They just called me from the city jail. They said they found Eldon Jones hanging in his cell. Would you meet me there?" She asked.

"I'll be there in a few minutes. You want me to pick you up?" he said.

"No, I've got a cab coming. I'll see you there," she said and hung up.

He went to Penny's office where she was putting the files on her desk.

"Maddie called. Eldon Jones hung himself at the jail. She asked me to come over there. Want to go along?"

"Let's go," she said. They went to the parking lot and he got into her cruiser with her. She drove across the city to police headquarters and parked in front. They went inside and to the cells in the back. The coroner was coming out, wheeling the covered body on a gurney. District Attorney, Walter Sugden, Lieutenant Winters and Chief Morrison were standing near the cell they found Jones in.

"What brings the new sheriff down here at this time of night?" Lieutenant Winters asked. Magee was about to respond when he heard Maddie speak from behind him.

"I asked him to come lieutenant. I'm going to request an independent investigation of Eldon Jones death. If you don't want the sheriff, I'll petition the attorney general to send some state people down here to do it," she said.

"I think the sheriff will be just fine," Chief Morrison said. "Is that all right with you Walt?" the chief asked the D.A.

"Sheriff Magee will be just fine, chief," Sugden said.

"Who found him?" Magee asked.

"The night jailor was making his check. He called for help and they got him down but he had been dead for some time," Winters responded.

"Well let's start with the jailor. Can we use a room for the interview?" Magee asked.

"Make yourself at home sheriff," the chief said. "I'm going home gentlemen. If you need me for anything, it can wait until morning. Winters and the D. A. soon followed the chief and went home.

Magee, Deputy Booker and Maddie talked with the jailer and everyone who had been in the jail during the night. Jones was last seen alive at 11:00 p.m. when the jailer walked by the cell and saw him asleep on his cot.

When he came back just before midnight, he was hanging from a strip of his blanket tied around his neck and around an iron bar in the window at the top of the wall. Magee went to the cell and stood inside the door. There was a metal bunk attached to one wall on his left. At the end of the bunk was a one-piece combination stool and sink made out of stainless steel. On the wall ahead of him was a window to the outside. It was located at the top of the wall, six feet off the floor. There was nothing on the wall to his right. Jones could not reach the bed or stool standing in front of the window. The jailer said his feet were off the ground more than a foot. The blanket strip had been removed before they got there. It was lying on the cot. He picked it up and examined the material. He tried to tear the material but couldn't it was to tightly woven. He looked closely at the strip and noted the strands of the weave had been cut with a sharp instrument. There is no way Jones pulled himself up a foot off the floor with this around his neck and the other end up around the bar. He kept his observations to himself, took the blanket strip and what was left of the blanket with him. He would have to wait for the coroner's report, he thought.

"Did he know of anyone else who was in here tonight?" he asked Penny.

"Just the ones we talked to," she responded.

"We'll come back in the morning and talk to the other prisoners," he said. He carried the blanket and walked out with Penny and Maddie.

Chapter 4

9:00 a.m. Tuesday
Jan. 5, 2000
Pueblo Police Headquarters

Sheriff Magee and Deputy Sheriff Penny Booker sat at the table in the large meeting room of the police department. The jailer who found Jones sat across the table from them.

"How bad did Jones get, after being locked up for two days?" Magee asked the jailer.

"What do you mean?"

"Was he sick? Drug withdrawal!"

"No. He looked all right to me. He wasn't sick."

"He didn't have DT's or the shakes?"

"No. He was as normal as any of the other prisoners."

"How many keys are there to his cell?"

"I carry a ring with all the cell keys. There's another ring in the desk in the squad room for the detectives to use and there is a spare ring kept in the store room." the jailer responded.

"Could you bring each of the prisoners in for an interview. The ones in the cells next to Jones," Magee said.

"There was only one. The other cells that were close to Jones were empty. We got one guy who is in for assault on his old lady. I'll get him," the jailer said.

"This is getting us nowhere," Penny said after the jailer left the room.

"I don't think we will find anything to tell us who murdered him," Magee said.

"You don't think it was suicide?"

"Like I said last night. Someone cut the blanket into that strip. There is no way Jones could have pulled himself up off the floor. Suicide victims will set up something to stand on, put the rope around their necks, then kick that something over. We'll see what the other prisoner knows, and then go over to the coroner's office," Magee said.

The jailer brought in a short thin Mexican and told him to sit.

"You know what happened to the man in the cell next to yours," Magee asked him. The man sat looking at Magee, not answering.

"Do you speak English?" he asked the man but didn't get any response.

"Does he speak any English?" he asked the jailer.

"I don't know. I never talked to him," the jailer responded.

"Is there anyone who speaks Spanish that can interpret for us?" Magee asked him.

"I don't know of anyone," he responded.

"Is Sergeant Lopez down on the desk?"

"Yes."

"Would you get him for us?"

"What about the prisoner?"

"I think we can watch him until you get back."

The jailer left the room and Magee lit a cigarette.

"Can you spare one of those for me?" the Mexican prisoner asked him in perfect English.

Magee handed him a cigarette then his lighter. He waited until he had the cigarette lit.

"Why pretend you don't speak English?" Magee asked him.

"They find out I can, I may not last longer than that black man did," the responded.

"Do you know what happened to the black man?" Magee asked.

"Every night since I've been in here, there's been too much light by the cells to get to sleep. Last night the lights were all off. I was sound asleep when I heard the cell door open. It was too dark to see who they were, but there were two of them. They put a garrote around his neck and strangled him. They cut the blanket into a rope and put it around his neck, then one lifted him up while the other one tied it off around the window bars," the prisoner said.

"Were they aware of you in the next cell?"

"Don't think so. When I saw the two figures go in, I slipped off the cot to the floor. It was pretty dark. I stayed down there until the jailer came by later and found the black man hanging up there," he said.

"Will you give us a statement in writing?"

"Are you crazy? They find out what I said, I'm a dead man."

"Can you tell us anything about the two?"

"No."

"Can't or won't?"

"They were both big. Neither of them had been in there before though. They kept bumping into everything in the dark."

"Did they say anything?"

"Not a word," the prisoner said. The door opened and Sergeant Patrick Lopez came into the conference room.

"Now you weren't out of here a day before they had to call you back for your expert help sheriff!" Lopez said in greeting.

"It's my curse. I thought I was rid of you people," Magee responded. "Do you speak Spanish?"

"Not a word, Jerry," Lopez said. "It is my curse to have the name Lopez and not speak my grandfather's language."

"Well, would you take this man back to his cell. We'll talk to him later," Magee said. Lopez motioned for the prisoner to stand and led him out of the conference room. Magee and Penny followed them out and left the building.

Penny drove her cruiser across town to the coroner's office and they went in looking for the medical examiner who worked on Eldon Jones.

He was sitting at a desk in one of the small offices outside the examination room. He told them he had just completed the examination of the body.

"He died of strangulation sheriff. I don't know why he had that strip of blanket around his neck. He was killed by something not much bigger than a wire. The markings around the neck are deep where the wire or small rope dug into the skin, deep enough to draw blood. There is a wide abrasion on the skin caused by the blanket but he was dead before he was hung," the doctor said.

"Did the toxoligy test show any illegal drugs?" Magee asked.

"Nothing. No sign of any drugs at all. He had some old needle tracks on his arms but they were several years old. I would say he was clean," he said.

"Anything out of the ordinary about the examination?" Penny asked.

"Pretty routine, oh yes, there was something strange. The undersides of the fingernails were scraped as we always do. His right hand had small specks of something I couldn't identify at first. Turns out it is make up. You know, flesh colored pancake make up like actors use. Not much, but enough to identify," the doctor said. Magee thanked the doctor and they left the building. They stopped off at a Burger King on the way to the office, to pick up some sandwiches. They took them to Magee's office and sat down at his desk to eat their lunch.

At 1:00 p.m., all of the deputy sheriffs were in the conference room when Penny took Magee in for their first meeting. She went around the room introducing each individual and Magee shook hands. There were three other women, which surprised him. Penny left Cline, Black and Dunn for last. They were all much younger than Magee expected. Cline was about six feet, slender and had a nice smile. Black was shorter and about thirty pounds heavier. His face had scar on one cheek, and he appeared to have a slight limp when he walked. Dunn was overweight. His uniform belt cut into his huge stomach. His face was fat and puffy. They all greeted him in a friendly manner, and then found their seats in the room.

Magee made a short speech and then told them he was going to hire some more help and was reorganizing the department. He said new assignments would be made in the coming days as they were worked out. Penny took over when he finished and covered some ongoing things then dismissed them. Magee returned to his office and sat down. He was about to pick up the phone when Emma told him he had a visitor. She moved out of the way and Mattie Patterson came in.

"Now I am going to stay right here until you sit down," he teased her.

"Good. My head still hurts. What did you find out about Eldon Jones?" she asked.

Magee told her of the conversation with the prisoner at the jail and the report from the coroner's office. She listened quietly until he finished.

"Well that would seem to wrap things up pretty well for whoever killed the late sheriff," she said.

Magee sat back in his chair appraising her. Her hair was down today. It caught the light as she talked, reflecting the reddish brown color. She had on a long winter coat, open in front and he saw she had on a green colored sweater. She looked good in sweaters. He couldn't see her below the waist, with the desk in the way, so he imagined what she looked like from the waist down. As if she read his mind, she stood up and walked across the room. Ah, he thought, same color matching skirt. Pleated skirt. Knee length. Nice legs. She stood staring at him, as if waiting for him to answer her.

"I'm sorry, what did you say?"

"I said I ran out of cigarettes could I borrow one of yours?"

He took the pack from his pocket and offered her one. He flipped his lighter and she took his hands as she leaned forward to light the cigarette. Her hands are soft, he thought.

"What are you doing for supper?" he asked.

"Back east they would call it dinner."

"Okay. What are you doing for dinner?"

"I hadn't looked ahead that far yet, why is this an invitation?"

"It is. I need to go by my place and clean up then I could take you out to eat."

"It's only four o'clock sheriff."

"Jerry. My friends call me Jerry."

"Very well Jerry, I'll have dinner with you but I have some work to finish up. Would you pick me up at my apartment at say 6:30?"

"I'll be there," he said. She left the office and he walked to the door to watch her go. Emma looked at him then turned to look at Maddie. She smiled as his eyes caught her's. He asked Emma if Penny was in. She said she would check and dialed her intercom. He went back into his office as his intercom buzzed. Emma told him that Penny was out somewhere in her car. He thought it was time to go find Dixie Flagg. He told Emma he would be out and would take a cruiser. He went to the parking lot and found four cars sitting there but had no idea where the keys were. He decided to take his Jeep and unlocked the door. He drove downtown and cruised the bars he knew Dixie worked late in the afternoon, looking for businessmen catching a quick drink before they went home.

He found her coming out of a rundown hotel on the west side. He stopped at the curb and she almost walked into the side of his car. She bent down to cuss out the driver and recognized him. He rolled down the window and invited her into the car.

"Word on the street is someone snuffed Eldon Jones," she said.

"Does anyone know who did it?" he asked her.

"The same someone who snuffed the late Orville Boone," she responded.

"I keep going around in circles on the Orville Boone killing, Dixie, and that circle brings me back to you. I have a feeling you were out at the Holiday Inn the night Boone was hit. I also have a feeling you know a lot more about it than you're telling. Now why is that?" Magee said.

"You going to get a nice looking uniform now sheriff or keep running around in those old worn out jackets?" she said.

"You're changing the subject Dixie. Does this jacket look that bad?" he said.

"Believe me. If you stay in plain clothes, invest in some new threads. You'd look grand in one of those sheriff's uniforms," she said.

"I need some help on this Dixie," he told her.

"I got a call that night from Boone. He sounded drunk like he always was. He told me to get my ass out to the motel so he could use it, his words exactly. He giggled like an idiot after he said it. I tried to tell him I was booked up. It made him mad. He told me to cancel and get out there."

"What time was that?"

"Somewhere around nine o'clock. I stalled as long as I thought I should. I figured maybe he would pass out if I waited. I took a cab and when I got there, Everett Cline saw me get out of the cab. He came charging out of the lobby and told me to get my sorry ass back into the cab and get out of there. I tried to explain that Boone sent for me, but he wouldn't listen. I got the hell out of there. It was really a relief. I couldn't stand that pig Boone. He liked to hurt me. Made him feel like a big man."

"Was Cline alone?"

"He's the only one I saw. He usually has Black and Dunn with him everywhere he goes but I didn't see them. There was something different about Cline though. He was out of uniform. I don't ever remember seeing him in regular clothes. He had on a short leather jacket, a sweatshirt and blue jeans. He seemed very upset. He yelled at me the moment he saw me."

"I need you to come down to my office and sign a statement about the money he collects from you. When can you do it?"

"You want to get me killed, I can't sign nothing."

"The only way we can put them out of business is get testimony from you and everyone else they're shaking down. It won't end until you help yourself."

She sat quietly for a moment, thinking about what he said. "Let me think about it. I've got a good appointment in a little while. I'll call you tomorrow," she said as she opened the car door and got out. She hurried down the sidewalk as though to get away before someone saw her with him.

Magee drove to his house and parked in the driveway. He walked up on the front porch and put his key in the lock. He turned the doorknob then remembered he left a pile of pending files on the front seat. The front door started to swing open as he started off the porch. He was on the last step down when the house erupted in a tremendous explosion. He felt a blast of hot air pick him up and toss him across the yard like a leaf in a windstorm. He landed very hard on the street by the curb, his head striking the concrete. His head was spinning and there was a terrific ringing in his ears. He tried to raise his head. He could barely see what was left of the house, flames leaping into the air. His Jeep was lying on its right side; oil around the transmission was burning, the flames crawling up the bottom of the vehicle. He tried to get up, then blackness took over and he passed out.

He came around and could hear voices mumbling. People were standing over him, talking to him, but they were jumbling the words. He couldn't understand them. Two faces appeared, pushing others away. One of the faces was talking to him, pulling at his clothes. He was lifted up and carried to a van or some truck like vehicle. He drifted in and out, feeling the movement of the truck. Blackness claimed him again.

Chapter 5

5:00 a.m. Thurs
Jan. 6, 2000
General Hospital

Magee returned to a conscious state. He knew he was awake but he couldn't get his eyes open. His eyelids were too heavy. He felt like he was floating. He felt like he was in a slow free fall from way up in the sky. Someone touched his arm. He managed to open his eyes. They wouldn't focus for a minute then he made out the outline of a face. He blinked his eyes. That was better. He blinked again and the face was all there. Penny Booker was looking at him. Good old Penny he thought. Lovely, competent, don't take no shit, Penny, was looking at him. Boy, I would like to be in bed naked with good old Penny. Shit, Penny's not old. Good young Penny.

Pretty, built like a brick shit house, young Penny. I would like to screw Penny, he told himself. When she spoke, it jolted him out of the drug-induced fantasy.

"You going to wake up boss?" she said. He looked at her for a few moments and finally managed to speak.

"What the hell happened?"

"Someone planted a bomb at your house. It was rigged to go off as you went through the front door but you managed to be off the porch when it blew. You know how you did that?"

"Unlocked the door and forgot files in the car. Started back to the car and kapow, up she went."

"You sound drunk. They must have you pumped full of pain medicine."

"Am I hurt bad?"

"You can't feel anything?"

"Not a thing. I feel like I'm floating."

"Well you look like shit. Your face is all scratched, lacerations the doctor calls them. Your jacket and shirt were shredded. Your neighbors found you on the street. Your T-shirt was full of little burning holes. They put them out. You have a severe concussion, and the explosion blasted the hell out of your ears. The doctor said you might have a problem hearing but that must have passed because you can hear me. He said you didn't have any broken bones, but you will be sore as hell for a few days. Your house and Jeep were totaled. I asked for help from the state bomb people. They came down and went through the ashes but didn't find much."

"I had a date. I'm late for my date."

"I know. Maddie is down in the waiting room. I'll get her in a minute. She came looking for you when you didn't pick her up. I picked out deputies I can trust and have them on the door of your room. They will rotate until we can get you out of here."

"Would you really do it?"

"Do what?"

"Kick my ass if I tried to screw you?"

"In a minute! How can you think of that in the shape you're in?"

"I think it's your body. You're very sexy. You have lovely boobs and your butt is unbelievable. Pretty face, great mouth, lovely eyes and soft skin."

"You're out of your head. I think your fantasies are coming to life and are flowing out of your mouth."

"Fantasies. Yes that's it. My fantasies. I think about screwing you all the time."

"Well put a sock in it. The nurse is coming," she said as an elderly woman came through the door.

"He's awake. How's he feeling?" the nurse asked.

"He's babbling like an idiot. Has he had a lot of morphine?" Penny asked.

"He had a shot for the burns when he first came in. It should be wearing off by now. It must be the concussion. It could make him delirious for a while," the Nurse said.

Magee listened to them as they talked and their voices started to blur as he slipped back into darkness again. He came around later and heard Maddie's voice talking to Penny, and then he slipped under again.

The pain in his head brought him around the next time. He opened his eyes to find daylight coming through the windows in his room. Christ his head hurt. He felt around on the bed for something to call the nurse. The door opened and a nice little old lady in a pink smock appeared. He spoke to her and she jumped and yelled from the surprise. He asked if she was a nurse. She mumbled she would get one.

"Can I get something for one bad headache?" he asked the nurse when she came in.

She turned around without a word and went back out the door. She came back carrying a cup with pills and a glass of water. He leaned up off the bed and took the pills, washing them down with water. The nurse cranked his bed up and he lay back, waiting for the pain to subside. He was dressed in just his shorts, so he checked himself over. There were abrasions and small burns on his chest. He felt his face and found more of the same. He slipped his feet out from under the sheet and let them hang over the edge of the bed. He slid down and stood up. He was dizzy at first, and then settled down. He went to the small room with the stool and sink. He pulled downs his shorts to go. The relief was tremendous. It had been hours since he took a piss.

When he finally finished and pulled his shorts back into place, he turned to walk back into the room. He was surprised to find Penny Booker standing by the bed watching him.

"It looks like that still works?" she said smiling at him.

"How long you been standing there?" he asked.

"Long enough! Can you get back in bed or do you need some help?"

"I can make it," he said. He sat down on the edge of the bed and slid across. He pulled the sheet up to his waist, more to hide what might develop than from modesty.

"What time is it? I don't know where my watch is?" he asked.

"It's about five in the afternoon. You're watch didn't make it through the blast. It must have hit the pavement as hard as your head did," she responded.

"When can I get out of here?"

"The doctor thought if you kept getting better, maybe in the morning. What are you going to need?"

"Clothes to start with. What about my uniforms?"

"They should be ready by Monday?"

"What day is this?"

"Thursday."

"I'll need some clothes then. What happened to my automatic?"

"I've got it. I found it lying on the grass halfway between what was left of the house and the street."

"It makes no sense!"

"What doesn't?"

"All this. Why kill Eldon Jones and why try to blow me up. We haven't found anything big enough to cause this. Everyone we talk to says Boone was small time. Why a bomb. It had to be someone who knew what they were doing. What about Winters and Morrison? They surely showed up on this. It's their jurisdiction."

"They all showed up and yes, they are investigating. They weren't too thrilled when I asked for help from the state boys but they did co-operate. Winters has been here at the hospital checking on you and your buddy the D.A. has been here twice. He sat down in the waiting room with Maddie for some time. You may have a rival there."

"Check on our errant deputies. I doubt if any of them had the smarts to make a bomb, but they are good suspects for the Jones killing. When you get the time, give the D.A. a report on what we know about it being a homicide instead of suicide and a copy to the police chief. Any idea where they put what was in my pockets?"

"Top drawer of the night stand there," she said pointing.

Magee opened the drawer and found his wallet. He took some money and gave it to Penny. She asked his sizes and told him she would do some shopping, then left.

At five thirty, an orderly brought him his supper. He was famished. He cleaned up the food and asked for more. He turned on the TV, hanging on the wall and was watching a situation comedy when Maddie came in.

"You go to great lengths to get out of a date," she teased him.

"I'm sorry I didn't show up. You had to think several things about why I wasn't there."

"I found Penny on her cellular phone. She told me you were in here. You were lucky. Who did this?"

"No idea, but I think we will find out. You look nice tonight, everything going okay at work?"

"It would be if I could get Eldon Jones off my mind. He certainly didn't deserve what someone did to him. How long do you have to be in here?"

"I should get out sometime tomorrow. When everything is back to normal, I'll try again for that supper date."

Before she could respond, Walter Sugden, the D.A. came into the room. He spoke to Maddie, and then turned his attention to Magee.

"I'm glad you finally woke up. How are you feeling?" Sugden asked.

"Not too bad."

"I saw the doctor down the hall. He thought they would kick you out of here in the morning. About the explosion, who would want to put you out of commission?"

"I have no idea. I haven't been sheriff more than one day so it can't be anyone I pissed off enough to kill me. I didn't have any cases with the city that would point to this either. Penny said you had been in before. I appreciate your concern."

"Like I told you, I need you in the sheriff's office. I won't stay long because you look tired. What can I get you?"

"Nothing thanks. Penny will get me some clothes."

"I'll take off then," Sugden said. "Nice to see you again Maddie."

"I should go too, Walt. I'll walk down with you. Take it easy Jerry. I'll check on you tomorrow," Maddie said then left with the D.A.

At 6:00 p.m. a nurse brought Magee his supper. He ate it all rapidly and still felt hungry. At 7:00 the doctor came in, checked over his chart and said he could go home in the morning.

"How about getting out of here tonight?" Magee asked. "It would throw off anyone watching the hospital."

The doctor understood what he meant and responded he would have his release ready in half an hour. Chief Deputy Penny Booker came through the door as the doctor left. She was carrying several packages and a shoebox.

"I talked the doctor into getting out of here tonight in case anyone is watching the place. What did you find for me to wear?"

"Enough to get you by until you can go shopping on your own." She showed him underwear, socks, shirts, blue jeans and a new pair of running shoes. He got out of bed and started dressing. When he was finished, she took a heavy jacket from the largest package. She picked up the packages with the rest of his new clothes as he took his personal items from the nightstand. When he was ready they left the room. The deputy by the door fell in behind them and they went to the nurse's station. He was checked out and the nurse went down to the lobby with them. Magee stayed by the door with the nurse and the deputy while Penny went to the parking lot and drove her cruiser out in front. He thanked the nurse and got in the front with Penny. The deputy went to his own cruiser and Penny called him on the radio and dismissed him for the night.

"Find me a good motel for the night and I'll start looking for a place tomorrow," he told her.

"I have a better idea for a few days until you can get something you want. Why not go out to the ranch. There is a lot of room in the ranch house. Charley Little Crow's wife lives out there with him and she can cook for you. Now before you answer, I already talked with Little Crow and his wife and they agreed," she said.

"Well then that is where we go," he said.

She drove south on the interstate. Magee rolled down the car window to feel what it was like outside. The sky was overcast with no stars in sight. The air felt damp and cold. He soon rolled the window back up.

It didn't take long to reach the ranch. The porch light came on as she parked by the gate out in front of the building. Penny grabbed his packages and he followed her up the walk to the front porch. Little Crow and his wife stood by the front door waiting for them. They welcome him and helped Penny with her packages.

"This is my wife Helen," Little Crow said introducing his wife. Helen was short and stocky. Her hair was dark black and she wore it in pigtails. She had a very pleasant smile and Magee liked her on first sight. She led him back down a hallway to a room at the back of the house. She showed him the connecting bathroom, and then took the packages Penny and her husband were carrying. She said she would put them away in the dresser the next morning. She took them all back through the house and into the kitchen. She told Magee that hospital food was all right for the sick, but she would bet he was hungry. He readily agreed with her. She told everyone to sit down and she served them sandwiches, salads and their choice of two different pies. Magee was ecstatic and ate like a hungry wolf. He was soon drinking his second cup of coffee and smoking a cigarette while Helen cleaned off the table. Penny insisted on helping and they were soon doing up the dishes.

"My only fear of staying with you two is the danger that might be following me around. The bad asses that tried to blow me up may try to get me out here," he said.

"We thought of that. Charley has a shotgun, an AR-16 and an automatic and knows how to use them. We are also scheduling a deputy with you full time until we get whoever is after you. I'm taking this watch. Helen will fix me up with a bedroom. Now we won't argue with you about this. It's already arranged," Penny said.

"I've only got one thing to say then!"

"What's that?"

"Can I have another piece of that pie?"

The next three weeks went by very fast for Magee. Charley Little Crow came to like him and he fell in love with Helen's cooking. He talked to Elmer Gray about paying the county some rent and worked out a deal to stay at the ranch. He also worked out a deal with Little Crow and his wife to share the grocery expense.

James Red Bear came to work for him and Penny assigned him as full time bodyguard to watch over Magee during the day. Other deputies were scheduled to trade off during the other shifts. Penny scheduled herself two or three nights a week and spent the night at the ranch when it was her turn.

Red Bear and Little Crow did not get started off very well. They hardly spoke at first. Magee worked on Little Crow to teach Red Bear how to ride the horses. After a week, they seemed to at least start talking to each other. By the second week, Little Crow had him on a quarter horse and things seemed to go better after that.

The changes in organization went into effect and Penny was successful in hiring three new deputies and four civilian employees.

Everett Cline, Joe Black and Glenn Dunn stayed away from Magee. Penny gave them their assignments and coordinated what had to be done with them.

Magee was very busy getting situated in his new position and learning his part in the court system as well as staying on top of the sheriff's responsibilities.

He spent the first part of each morning reviewing the calls that came in, what deputies were assigned to complaints, reports on contacts and case files if the response merited a file being started. He was called to the scene of anything deemed very important. Chief Deputy Penny Booker and his secretary Emma White were an enormous amount of help to him. They both handled the many details of the work and anticipated what he would need or need to do in about every situation. The only thing that was not getting done was much progress on the Orville Boone and Eldon Jones murder cases.

Penny was getting nowhere on anything substantial concerning the three deputies Cline, Black and Dunn. Magee had talked with the state police experts about the bomb at his house. They found little of the device that triggered the explosion. They found traces of a plastic explosive and identified it but came up with nothing on where it came from. Penny and Magee were as puzzled by the lack of progress as much as they were about why no one had come after the sheriff since the explosion.

Magee's insurance company had settled on the house and its contents and on the car. Penny helped him buy more clothing and personal items. He put off buying a car as he finally got his own department cruiser.

He saw little of Maddie Patterson. Penny said she saw her with Walt Sugden at a steak house one evening. Magee wasn't too disappointed as he was about as busy as he could get.

Chapter 6

7:00 a.m. Tuesday
Feb. 1, 2000
Sheriff's Office

It was spitting light snow when Magee left the ranch to drive into the office. By the time he parked in the lot and walked to the building, it was coming down fairly heavy. The wind was picking up and the temperature was going down. He brushed the snow off his coat in the office and hung it on the rack. He went to the coffee pot in the squad room and poured a cup, then returned to his office and sat down at his desk. The phone rang; the dispatcher was on the line.

"The sheriff from Ouster County is on line one," she told him. He picked up the phone and pushed the button.

"Jerry, this is Bill Nash. We got a call last night from a family in San Isabel about a missing boy. The kid is ten years old. We sent a deputy out there last night and the boy hasn't been located. We're organizing a search around the area and I wondered if you could spare some help to look east of the town over in your county?"

"No problem Bill. I'll send some deputies over. Where can they meet you?"

"Tell them to go to the town hall. We'll organize there. We may not get far today. This storm seems to be getting worse. Appreciate the help. I'll check in later on how we do," the sheriff said then hung up. Magee punched the intercom for Penny's office.

"Bill Nash has a small boy missing in San Isabel. He's asking for some help. Send three or four of the troops over there. Tell them to take the four-wheel drive vehicles and warm clothes. Check in at the town hall. Tell them to keep in touch with the dispatcher and to be careful with this storm getting worse," he told her.

"I'll send three in each Jeep. I hope the kid is in some kind of shelter. It's damn cold out there today," she responded.

Magee was busy the next two hours, but kept being distracted, thinking about the search going on in the southwest part of the county.

He finally left the office and went looking for Penny. He found her in the dispatcher's office.

"Nothing yet. It's tough going, little visibility with the wind blowing the snow around. The snow is piling up which confines them to the roads. They can't get too far out into the open areas," she said.

"Do we have any more four wheel drive vehicles?" he asked.

"A brand new Bronco, but it's out on patrol."

"Call it in. I'm not getting anything done in here. I'll go out and help with the search."

"I'll go along. You will get lost," she said. Before he could respond she told the dispatcher to call the deputy in the Bronco and tell him to come in and get a different car.

Magee went to his office and put on his heavy coat. He met Penny at the back door. She wore a heavy coat with a hood and was pulling on her gloves. The deputy drove up to the door and turned the Ford over to them. Penny got in behind the wheel and drove out of the parking lot.

"The only thing wrong with this rig is they haven't installed the radios yet," Penny told him. "I've got my portable cellular but I don't think we will have much range in this storm."

She drove south on the interstate and made good time. Visibility was poor at times but she had two lanes to stay on the road. Near the south border of the county she turned west on State 165 that led to San Isabel. It was harder to see driving west and the snow was starting to pile up in drifts.

The Bronco broke through the soft snow okay but Magee was wondering about getting through the drifts later on.

San Isabel was a small town sitting just inside the foothills that began to rise up from the plane toward the mountains. On a clear day one could see Greenhorn Mountain south and a little west of the town.

At the west edge of the foothills a county road intersected the state highway. Penny took the wrong turn in the blowing snow and they were now going north when they thought they were still on the road for San Isabel. They went over a mile when they came to an open stretch of road and discovered the surface was not asphalt.

"I think I got us lost," Penny said.

"Watch out!" Magee yelled as a stalled pickup suddenly appeared on the road ahead of them.

Penny got the Bronco stopped just short of the pickup. It was stuck in a fair sized snow bank. They could see someone through the back window of the cab.

"Stay with the car. I'll check on them," he told her as he pulled the hood of his coat over his head and tied it tight. He struggled out the door and up to the pickup. He went to the passenger side and opened the door. Penny could see he was talking with whoever was in the cab. He then reached inside and when he came back into view he was carrying a young boy. He hurried as well as he could through the snow to the Bronco. She reached over and opened the door for them. Magee slid the boy in on the front seat, shut the door and started back to the pickup. He went around to the driver's side and opened the door. In a few moments the driver got out and Magee followed him back to the Ford.

He opened the back door for the man, waited until he was in, and then shut the door and climbed back in front with Penny and the boy.

"I think we found our lost boy. This young man is Eddie Nelson and that man in back is his Father, Eddie Sr. It seems Eddie and his wife have been divorced for several years and there has been a running custody battle.

Eddie picked the boy up on the street last night and started to take off with him. The boy talked him out of it and his dad tried to get him back home. He took the wrong turn like we did. See if you can get turned around and head back south and we'll see if we can find the highway.

"How long you two been stuck in that drift?" Penny asked the boy.

"Long enough to run out of gas," the man in the back answered. "I guess we were lucky you came out here. We might have froze to death in there if we had to stay all night."

"You okay Son," Magee asked the boy. "You aren't hurt?"

"I'm okay. My daddy would never hurt me, would you dad?" the boy said.

His father didn't answer and there was little more said on the ride into town. Penny found the highway and twenty minutes later they were parked in front of the town hall.

A sheriff's cruiser and one of their Jeeps sat at the curb. They took the boy and his father inside. A woman let out a yell when she saw the boy, running to him, hugging and kissing him. Bill Nash was right behind her. Magee took him aside and told him what he got from the boy's father. Nash thanked him for finding them and for all the help in the search. Penny, Magee and the deputies left the hall and went to their vehicles.

"He's going to call the other Jeep and send them back. We'll follow these guys back and see if that Jeep can break us a trail to follow," Penny told him.

They had a hard time seeing the Jeep ahead of them but neither of them could move very fast, breaking through the deep snow. They barely made it to the interstate. The Jeep got stuck on the on ramp and had to back out and hit the drift at a pretty good speed to get through. They did bust the drift enough for the Bronco to get through behind them.

State snow plows had been by on the interstate and it was clear enough to drive as fast as the visibility would allow.

"It was sheer luck that we found that pickup," Penny said.

"They said that road had been searched earlier and they found nothing. They couldn't have been stuck there very long. You're right it was luck. I guess we were supposed to take the wrong turn and find them," Magee said.

"If we go back to the office, you will have to spend the night in the city. The road to the ranch will be blocked," she said. "Oh shit!" she exclaimed. A semi had jack knifed across both lanes ahead of them. The Jeep with the three deputies must have been close when it slid. The Jeep was on the right shoulder lying on its side. Penny was all over the highway stopping the Bronco, but managed to miss the Jeep. They stopped just short of the semi. The driver of the big truck was outside, trying to open the driver side front door of the jeep. Magee jumped out, and ran to help him. He struggled up onto the vehicle and pulled the door up. He yelled for the driver to keep it open. He dropped down into the Jeep. One deputy was lying on the right passenger door, the other two were balled up in the back. The man in front was unconscious, his face bloody from the broken windshield. One deputy in the back was conscious and struggling to get free from the other man. Magee spoke to him. He responded and said he was okay but his buddy looked like he was hurt bad.

Magee struggled with the man in front. He worked around behind him, got him under his arms and pulled him upright. He grabbed him around the waist and pushed him up through the open door and onto the top of the Jeep. The driver wrenched the door back, breaking the latch so the door would stay open. He grabbed the deputy and drug him down to the ground. Magee went back for the other two. He told the man in back to help him work the unconscious deputy into the front seat. When he had him where he could get a hold of him, he pushed him up and out the same way. The third deputy was able to crawl up and out by himself. Magee boosted himself up and then dropped off the vehicle. Penny and the driver of the semi were carrying the first deputy to the Bronco. The second man was lying on the pavement. Magee and the third deputy picked him up and started for the Bronco. They soon had both of the injured men in the back and the third deputy in the front seat.

"Can you move the truck enough to get it around and out of the lane of traffic?" Magee asked the driver.

"I can try," the man said.

The driver backed the big truck up a few feet, and then drove forward, working the steering wheel back and forth as he tried to get straightened out on the road. After what seemed like forever, he had it headed north again. Magee ran up beside him and climbed up on the step as he opened the door.

"Try to get to Pueblo. You'll have to hole up for tonight. Find the sheriff's station and we'll get the accident report filled out. Thanks for helping get them out," he told the driver. He ran back to the Bronco and got in front. Penny was talking on her small phone. She started the Bronco moving the moment he was inside. They soon lost sight of the semi ahead of them, but she pushed the Bronco up to thirty-five, hoping he kept moving.

"I got the dispatcher. She's calling the hospital to warn them we're coming in with two injured. She didn't think she could get a car out here very soon to work the accident. I told her the Jeep was off the road far enough that it wasn't a hazard for now. I told her when the storm lets up, to get a car down here and a wrecker. How are those two doing?" she said.

Magee had leaned over the seat back and was checking on both of the injured men. One was still out, while the other was coming around. He was moaning with pain. The deputy in the seat between them seemed to be in shock.

"I think they will all make it in if we don't run into anything. The bleeding has stopped but he's unconscious. I think this one has a broken arm. Hell, I don't remember any of their names," Magee said.

"We're coming into the city. The wind is not quite as strong here. I can see about half a block," Penny said as she picked up the speed a little. Fifteen minutes later she turned off on a ramp and then turned again on a cross street. Five minutes later she was pulling up to the emergency entrance of the hospital.

Several of the hospital staff came out on the run. They helped get the injured men out and on gurneys. They rushed them all inside with Penny and Magee following.

They stood outside the treatment rooms as the doctors worked on the men, then moved to a waiting room where they sat down on a soft couch. Magee was exhausted. Let down from the adrenaline rush he thought. He wasn't aware of falling asleep. It was two hours later when he felt Penny shaking him. He was lying flat on his back on the couch. He opened his eyes and at first felt embarrassed that he had fallen asleep.

"How are they?" he asked her.

"None of them are very bad. Kevin Reddinger was driving. He's the one who hit the windshield. He had a bad concussion. The second one unconscious in the back was Freddy Reese. He had a broken arm. He was knocked cold but the doctor said he don't think he has too bad a concussion. The guy we thought wasn't hurt at all, Donny Littig, had three broken ribs and was in shock. They have them all stable now. The doctors said they would all be okay. You're pretty strong when things get exciting. You brought those two out of there like they didn't weigh a thing," she said.

"Had to be adrenaline. When I relaxed, I fell asleep," he responded.

"Let's go find some supper," she said.

"What time is it?"

"Almost eight o'clock."

They found the Bronco in a parking lot, covered with snow. The storm had not abated any. If anything, it seemed to be getting worse. Penny started the Ford and they plowed through the drifts, heading back out onto the street. She reached a through street where city snowplows had recently been, and they moved along faster. The visibility was still bad, but after a twenty-minute drive, Penny pulled up into the driveway of her house and parked the car in front of the garage. Magee followed her through the drifts to the front door. She fumbled with her keys, and then unlocked the door and they both went in.

Magee was impressed at what he saw. The front door opened into a large family room with thick carpet, sofas, easy chairs, a large television set and floor to ceiling patio doors at one end.

She led him back through a hall, and then turned left to an open entry with two bedrooms and adjoining baths. She opened the door to the unoccupied bedroom and said he could sleep there. She led him back across the hall to the kitchen.

"How do scrambled eggs, ham and toast sound?"

"Fine. Chasing around in a blizzard makes me hungry."

"You make some coffee and I'll get started as soon as I get out of these wet clothes. You look like your pants are soaked."

"They are but they will dry," he said as he looked through the cupboards for the coffee. The water was running through the ground coffee when she came back. She was wearing an old faded pair of blue jeans and a sweatshirt. She was carrying a pair of sweat pants. She tossed them to him.

"These were my brother's. They look like they should fit. Go get out of those wet pants," she told him.

He went across to the bedroom and took off his clothes. He went into the bathroom and looked in the medicine cabinet for something of her's to borrow to shave with. The cabinet was empty. He went to her bedroom, then into the bathroom and found a disposable razor and some shaving soap. Stuff she uses on her legs, he thought. He went back into his bathroom and started to shave. He stood in his shorts, looking at his face. The cuts from the explosion were about healed but he had to shave around them to keep from causing them to bleed. He ran his hands through his thick dark hair, touching two of the abrasions. They seemed to be about healed up. He carefully put on the soap and shaved. He was about finished when he saw Penny standing in the doorway watching him.

"Your eggs are going to get cold."

"Be right there. I'll take a bath after we eat."

He washed off the soap, pulled on the sweats over his shorts and put his T-shirt back on. He joined her at the kitchen table where she had their plates ready. He studied her face as he ate, enjoying the beauty he saw.

"Where does your dark skin come from?"

"Well, there are two versions passed down through the family. The first story was that my great, great grandmother was Polynesian. My great, great grandfather was an English ships captain who found her in the Pacific somewhere, married her and took her back to England. The second story was that he married an Egyptian princess and lived out the rest of his life in Egypt. No one ever verified either story. This was on my mother's side of the family. She has dark skin too and she is beautiful," Penny said.

"Where is she?"

"She and my father live back east in Maine. My father was a college professor who is now retired. They have a nice place. I don't get back to see them much," she said. "What about you. Magee is a Jewish name isn't it?"

"Well there are probably two stories there too. I'm supposed to be descended from Jewish heritage back two or three generations but there was an Irish spelling of the name with a Mc in front instead of Mag. I always thought I was probably an Irish Jew," he responded.

"Your family didn't practice the Jewish faith?"

"My mother said they did a long time ago. I don't know where we fell off the track but my parents were Presbyterians. My dad's gone now. My mother lives in Omaha and like you, I don't go see her enough."

"You were in the army?"

"Twenty years!"

"Your not old enough to be a twenty year soldier."

"I'm thirty seven, almost thirty eight. I went in at seventeen. Retired a major. How old are you?"

"Thirty one!"

"How come you aren't married?"

"How come you aren't?"

"I asked first!"

"Okay, I've dated different guys. I'm no virgin. I lost that way back during my first year in college. I guess I never found anyone who I felt comfortable with," she said. She also added, "until now," in her mind. "What's your story?"

"Why I'm still a virgin. Women scare me to death!" he teased her.

"In a pig's eye," she responded.

"I dated a few girls in high school. Several one-night stands in the army. I guess I never slowed down long enough to establish any kind of a relationship with a woman," he said, also adding "until now," in his mind.

"You want some more coffee?" she asked, getting up.

"Please, what about the men in the hospital. I never thought about notifying their families about the accident."

"I called the dispatcher to handle it. Reddinger and Reese are married. The dispatcher was going to send someone out with the other Jeep to take their wives to the hospital. Littig is single. His parents live in Ohio. The dispatcher was going to call them. We need to check on them in the morning on the way in to the office," she said.

"You are very efficient, now for that bath. The eggs were good. Someone taught you how to cook?"

"My mother. Save the water when you're done and I won't have to run another tub."

Magee went to the window and looked outside. He could see the snow blowing by a streetlight out on the street. He went across to the bathroom and started the water running in the tub. He took off the sweats and his underwear and sat down in the hot water. He leaned back, his head on the end of the tub, and closed his eyes.

"You fall asleep in there, you will drown," he heard her say. He opened his eyes. She was standing in front of the mirror over the sink, a large towel wrapped around her.

He reached for the washrag and dropped it over his groin. Automatic modesty, he thought after he did it. Her back was to him, and he examined her backside. Her legs were beautiful. The towel came down to just below the curve of her butt.

His mind automatically went into fantasy mode, imagining what the butt looked like under the towel.

"Are you going to be in there all night. I want to wash up!"

"Sorry, I was distracted!"

"I could see the frost start to cover your eye balls. I keep forgetting to ask why you told me to reassign Red Bear. You still need someone watching your back."

"It's been some time since the bomb went off. Whoever did it may have backed off, since we are not getting very close right now. We need to get back on both cases. I think we should put Red Bear to work on it full time. Besides, I figure you're watching my back," he responded.

"Yell when you get out," she said as she went out the door.

He stood up and reached for a bath towel and dried off. He put his shorts and T-shirt on then stepped into the sweat pants. He went out through his bedroom and across to hers, telling her he was finished. He went on into the living room, turned on the television set. He sat down on a couch and lit a cigarette.

It was ten o'clock and the news was on. The weatherman was predicting that the storm would move off during the night and tomorrow would be cold. There was a local story about the missing boy in San Isabel and the report that he had been found. There was film of the boy and his mother. Magee wondered how they got that, with the storm going on. He didn't notice Penny coming in to join him but felt the couch give as she sat down beside him. She wore a terry cloth robe, a towel wrapped up around her hair. She pulled her feet up under her, took the towel loose and rubbed her hair to dry it. Her hair was dark black. She wore it short, above the shoulders. It seemed to shine, reflecting the light from the television, the only light in the room. The robe opened at the bottom enough for him to see part of her legs, from the knees up.

His imagination took over and he wondered what it would feel like to run his hand over the inside of her legs, across the smooth skin, moving toward the dark patch of hair that had to be there, where her legs ended and her smooth stomach began. The top of the robe was tight up around her neck but he could see the outline of her breasts pushing on the material. He looked up and caught her eyes with his. He blushed at being caught staring. She smiled and stared back, studying his profile. His face was very pleasant, a handsome face with thick black eyebrows over eyes that seemed to always be busy, a wide, straight nose and full lips. White even teeth when he smiled. She looked down his chest where she could see dark hair through the thin T-shirt, on down to his crotch, the bulge showing. Pushing up the cotton material of the sweat pants then on down to his bare feet. She felt a warm glow between her legs. What happens to our working relationship if I get him in bed, she wondered? She had fantasies of him lying beside her naked, his hands caressing her between her legs, over her breasts. Her breathing increased as she thought about it.

"You want something to drink?" she said to break the spell.

"What have you got?"

"There should be some Canadian Club in the kitchen. Sour or sweet?"

"Sour. Squirt if you have any?" he responded.

She left the couch and went to the kitchen. He flipped through the channels with the remote control. He found an old movie and leaned back to watch. She came back with two glasses and handed him his drink. She sat down again, automatically pulling her legs up under her.

They sat watching the movie, nursing the drinks. The whisky spread through Magee with a warm feeling and he became drowsy. He sat his glass down and relaxed. As his head drooped, he sat up, fighting sleep. She reached over to him and gently pulled him down until his head was in her lap. He brought his feet up and spread out on the couch. He was soon asleep, snoring softly.

She ran her hand over his chest and down his stomach, feeling his muscle under the skin. The excitement of the day and the drink caught up with her and she fell asleep too. Sometime during the night she woke to find she was lying on the couch with Magee up tight behind her, his arms wrapped around her. She carefully worked herself loose and went to the bathroom. She brought a blanket back and covered him, then went to her bedroom and went to sleep in her own bed.

Chapter 7

6:00 a.m. Wed.
Feb. 2, 2000
Dep. Sheriff Booker's House

Magee woke up slowly, his bladder telling him he had to get up soon. He went to the bathroom, and then looked in on Penny. She was softly snoring, the blankets pulled up around her neck. It was cold in the house. He went back to his bedroom and dressed, then to the kitchen to make coffee. He went to the window and could see the storm had blown itself out. It had stopped snowing and he could see it was going to be a clear day.

He poured some coffee and sat at the kitchen table, lit a cigarette and thought about the night before, dreaming of what might have been. He was certainly attracted to Penny. Every time she was in his sight, he felt a warm sensation in his stomach. He wondered if he should be more aggressive. He drifted off into a fantasy again, picturing her naked in his mind. He jumped when she spoke to him.

"The coffee smells good. You ready for breakfast?" she said as she came into the kitchen.

"I never pass up someone cooking for me. I hate to cook. The storm's over, maybe we can get out on the highway and haul the Jeep back into town," he said.

She cooked them breakfast, and then they bundled up in their winter coats and went outside to dig the snow off the Bronco. They backed through the drifts in the driveway and found that snowplows had opened the street. Penny drove to the hospital so they could check on the deputies. They found all three up and eating breakfast. They visited with them and the wives, and then moved on to the office.

Penny left him to go to her desk, telling him she would send someone for the Jeep. He went to his office, finding Emma White at her desk, busy with her paper work. Responding to her questions, he filled her in on their trip through the storm.

He went through the reports on his desk, then the mail. He was thinking about locating Red Bear when he came walking into the office.

"Those guys in the Jeep were lucky, it could have been bad," Red Bear said. "Dispatch said you and Booker found the boy?"

"More luck. We found him with his father, stuck in a snow bank," Magee responded. "What has Penny got you doing?"

"Patrol mostly. Serving a few papers."

"How about concentrating on our unsolved murder cases for awhile?"

"We have detectives that should be doing that," Red Bear responded.

"And getting nowhere," Magee said. "Sit down and go over the Boone case with me. You were there from the start. Have you been through the file?"

"The medical examiner's report said they found two .25 caliber slugs. The one in his head didn't go clear through. Small caliber makes me think of a woman's gun," Red Bear said.

"That's not a whole lot to say it was a woman."

"There was no sign of forced entry. He had a reputation of meeting women at motels. He expected whoever shot him. He let her in."

"The desk clerk said he was pretty drunk."

"Pretty drunk is relative to different people. If he was a hard drinker, he could function with a lot of booze in him."

"What about Dixie Flagg. She got a call from him demanding that she come to the motel and service him. She said she saw Cline at the motel who chased her away."

"He might have been expecting Dixie and some other woman was at the door when he opened it."

"Spend the next few days concentrating on Boone's file. Find Dixie and have another talk with her. Pay particular attention to Cline, Black and Dunn. I don't feel very secure with those three around. It's like sending the fox to guard the chicken house. Go back out and interview Boone's widow again. Follow everything up again. We need a break on this," Magee said.

Red Cloud stood up, nodded his head and left. Magee followed him out and went looking for a cup of coffee. He found Penny in the coffee room.

"The Jeep has been picked up and is on the way in. Most of the roads are open now. You should be able to get to the ranch," she said.

"I put Red Cloud on the Boone file full time. Try and monitor his progress and give him what help he might need," Magee told her. They went their separate ways, Penny to organize the day's activities and Magee to his pile of paper work.

Deputy Sheriff James Red Bear started his special assignment by driving out into the countryside to visit Orville Boone's widow. The sun was out and the sky was clear. The roads had all been plowed. Red Bear pulled into the long drive at the Boone ranch, following a tractor with a blade cleaning the snow. He parked in front of the large house, climbed out of his cruiser and watched the man in the tractor as he plowed the snow around the large circled drive. He walked to the front door and rang the bell. He was surprised at the nice looking woman who opened the door.

"Good morning Mrs. Boone. I'm with the Pueblo Sheriff's Department. I wonder if I could ask you a few questions, to follow up on our investigation into your husband's murder?" he politely asked her.

"You're Red Bear. Magee took you with him when he moved into the sheriff's office. Come in. You're wasting your time out here. I told them everything I know. You want some coffee?" she said.

"If it's not too much bother," he responded.

"No bother for me, I have a maid to do that work. Come in deputy, we'll go out to the family room," she said. She led him through the house to a large room with one entire wall of glass. The view from that side of the room was spectacular. The mountains in the distance were covered with snow. She motioned for him to sit in one of the easy chairs and the maid brought them coffee.

"You people don't seem to be getting anywhere with Orville's case," she said.

"It's not from a lack of trying Mrs. Boone. We don't have a lot to work with," he responded.

"Mrs. Boone is too formal deputy. Call me Eloise. What is your given name?"

"James. Jimmy is what I hear the most."

"Then I'll call you Jimmy. You're a full-blooded Indian. I never knew any full-blooded Indians. You're not bad looking either. How old do you think I am?"

"I couldn't even guess," he responded, going along with the conversation.

"Forty Six. Ten years younger than Orville was. I can't remember the last time I slept with the old bastard before he got his. Women have needs too Jimmy. I could have given him some of his own medicine. I could have found a lover. Don't know why I didn't."

"How much did you know about his illegal activities?"

"Plenty. I think it was common knowledge that he made everyone pay him protection money. He wasn't the brain though. He wasn't smart enough to keep everything running. He just did what she was told."

"Who was telling him what to do?"

"I never found out. He got phone calls at all times of the day and night, a man's voice. He got mad as hell when I answered the phone. Said it was business."

"Did this individual ever come to the house?"

"Not that I ever knew of. He was the reason Orville drank so much. I don't know what his excuse was for chasing all the hookers."

"Did he keep any records here at the house? Any paper work, books or ledgers?"

"He had an office next to his bedroom. I never went near the room. We can go take a look if you think there may be something we can use," she told him. She stood up and led him back through the house to the large bedroom where her husband slept. She opened a door that led into a smaller room. Inside was a desk, bookshelves along one wall and two file cabinets. Red Bear sat down at the desk and started going through drawers. He found very little. Under the desk, he found three buttons attached to the wood. He pushed one and a panel slid back on the opposite wall. He looked at Eloise, her eyes wide in surprise. The panel hid a large television screen. He pushed the second button and the set turned on. He pushed the third button and a VCR tape started playing. Red Cloud's mouth dropped open at what started playing on the screen. A man lay on a bed nude. A naked woman was crawling up onto the bed. She took him in her mouth and proceeded to perform fellatio on him. Red Bear stared in amazement, thinking he should shut it off, yet not wanting to. The woman was soon on top of the man, gyrating her hips with wild abandon. He was about to stop the tape when Eloise told him to leave it on. He wanted to turn it off or get out of the room as it was turning him on. He looked at her and saw it was having the same effect on her.

The tape abruptly ended and a new tape started. It was the same bedroom, different woman, and different man. The woman was on her back in the missionary position, the man on top, pumping to his hearts delight. Red Bear hit the button to shut it off.

"Why that dirty old son of a bitch," she said. "There had to be some blackmail involved there somewhere."

"Did you recognize anyone you know?"

"No, but there appears to be a lot more to look at."

Red Bear proceeded to search all the drawers in the desk. He found nothing connected to what Boone may have been into. There were half a dozen VCR tapes lying beside the VCR player.

"Could I take these along to view? I need to see if the people can be identified."

"Help yourself," she said. She went to the desk and hit the play button. The screen came alive with the two on the bed in wild lovemaking. A few minutes later, this tape stopped and a new scene came on. The first woman was back with a new man. She was on her hands and knees on the bed, the man on his knees behind her, shoving his hips rapidly.

Red Bear was about to say something to Eloise but hated to interrupt the pleasure she seemed to be getting from watching. He turned his attention to the file cabinets and was not aware when she left the room. He turned to speak to her and she was gone, the tape still playing. He crossed the room to turn it off but before he could reach the desk he heard her speak to him.

"Christ it's been a long time!" she said, standing in the open doorway with nothing on. Red Bear was shocked and stimulated at the same instant. She was very well put together. She crossed the room and pushed up against him. She put one hand behind his neck and pulled his mouth down to hers. Her mouth was on fire. He was so amazed; he just stood with his eyes open until she found his tongue with hers. Instant response. He started to become hard and responded to her kiss. She was fumbling with his zipper and soon had her hand on him. He reached down, picked her up and carried her to the bed in the next room. What she did to him could be considered rape but he didn't struggle very much. She kept him on the bed for over two hours, taking her pleasure as she gave in kind. When she was finally satisfied and lay back on the bed, he put his clothes on. He went into the office and shut off the tape player, gathered up all the tapes and came back to the bedroom.

"Feel free to stop out anytime you think you may need to talk to me again," she said.

"I'll do that," he responded, smiling at her as he went out of the bedroom. He was smiling all the way to the car.

Red Bear drove back to the city and to the last known address he had on Dixie Flagg. She lived in a four-story apartment building that had seen better days. He rode the elevator up to the third floor and was surprised when she answered the door.

She stood with the security chain still attached, the door open just a few inches. She looked like he woke her up, sleep still in her eyes. She had a well-worn robe wrapped around her.

"I'm Jimmy Red Bear, Dixie. I work for Jerry Magee. He suggested I come talk to you about anything you may have remembered about Orville Boone," he said.

She stood staring at him, trying to decide whether to let him in. She unlatched the chain and pulled the door open. He followed her in, looking the place over. It was a small studio apartment with the bed in the largest room. She plopped down on the bed. He pulled a chair over and sat down. Her robe was struggling to cover her but was losing the battle.

"I talked with Boone's widow. She seemed to think there was someone pulling the late sheriff's chain, someone who told him what to do. Did you ever pick up on anything like that?"

"I don't know anything about him having a boss. I wouldn't doubt it though. He was too damn dumb to put things together himself," she responded.

"I found some tapes at his house. Could I show you a part of one to see if you recognize anyone? I should warn you, they are sexually graphic," he said.

"Like that's supposed to upset me. I'll take a look. There's a VCR on the shelf under the TV over there," she said pointing to a corner of the room.

Red Bear turned on the VCR and the TV set and put the tape in. He picked one from random. The picture that came on showed a couple in bed, the woman on top, her eyes closed, was moving rapidly and moaning. Red Bear recognized the woman immediately. It was Dixie. Before he could think, he glanced from the screen to her sitting on the bed, then back at the screen.

"Why that no good son of a bitch. He had a camera set up," she yelled.

"Where was that taken?"

"The Holiday Inn on the interstate. There are three rooms reserved for all the girls that work out there. I'll bet the bastard had a camera in every room."

"You know the man in the tape?"

"He's a nobody, just some John. You look at all those tapes and you're going to find some important people though. That old shit had to be blackmailing them," she said. The tape stopped and a new man and women appeared.

"That's Shirley. Boy she will be pissed when she finds out about this."

"How many different women will be on the tapes?"

"Probably twelve, all of us girls who have been kicking back part of our take. Talking about the take, something strange has been going on," she said.

"What's that?"

"No one has been around to collect since Orville got himself killed."

Red Bear left Dixie talking to herself about the tapes and drove back to the office. He took the tapes inside and put them down on Magee's desk. He explained what was on them and told about his talk with Mrs. Boone. He left out the part about the workout on the bed. He also told about showing one of the tapes to Dixie and who was on the tapes. Magee sat grinning while he talked.

"I know it will be tough duty, but find someplace private to review all of the tapes. We need to know who all the male clients are. You don't have to do it in one sitting. Spread it out over several days," the sheriff told him.

Red Bear picked up the tapes and left the office, shaking his head. It was fifteen minutes later before the grin faded from Magee's face, and only then when his mind went on to other work.

Chapter 8

8:00 p.m. Fri.
Feb. 4, 2000
Boone, Colorado

Boone, Colorado is a small town located north of the Arkansas River at the junction of highways 96 and 50, some twenty miles or so east of Pueblo. The town was too small to have city services and looked to the county sheriff's office for law enforcement.

A mile north and a half mile east of town, sat a large old bunkhouse built years ago as sleeping quarters for hired hands working on the Boone ranch. The ranch house, barn and other buildings were long gone. Burned down or rotted to the point they just fell in. Seventy or eighty years ago it had been a prosperous ranch with several thousand cattle. Orville Boone's grandparents owned it. It passed to Orville's parents who had no interest in it. Over the years, most of the land had been sold off until there was just a few acres were the building set.

The bunkhouse was back from the county road and screened by a row of trees. The activity at the place the past few months was not noticed by anyone that didn't know what was going on there.

Michael Enserro drove his beat up old Chevy pickup down the county road looking for the driveway to the bunkhouse. Michael was the Mexican spending the night in jail in the next cell with Eldon Jones the night he was killed. The official charge had been beating his wife around. He pled guilty the next day on a simple assault charge, paid the fine and was released. Enserro was not what he seemed.

Getting into the city jail had been carefully planned. Enserro was a sergeant in the Mexican Federal Police. He was in Colorado on an unofficial quest, looking for the daughter of his older brother. Tina Enserro was only fifteen. She was headstrong and independent. She left home with the dream of going to the United States and getting a good job or a rich husband. Tina developed early and looked much older than her fifteen years. She was very attractive and very naive. It had taken her uncle six months to find out she had paid a gringo to smuggle her into the country. She was reported to have made it as far as Pueblo, Colorado, and then she disappeared.

Enserro spent a considerable amount of time in the cheap saloons frequented by the many migrant workers who came to pick the fruit at harvest time. Many of them stayed, waiting for the next harvest. He was about to give up his search, when he overheard a young man bragging about the nice looking whores at the bunkhouse. The young man had too much to drink and told of when he first came to Colorado last fall to pick peaches. He said he went to the whorehouse with the other men and was surprised at the quality of the young women. He said he had just gone back out there last night and they were still there and were still in business. Enserro bought the man more to drink and found out the location of the place.

As he drove up the driveway, he saw lights in the windows of the long structure. He parked in front and walked to the door, and inside the building. He was in a small waiting room. A counter off to his left had a sign over a bell, announcing ring for service. He rang the bell and a heavyset woman came waddling up to the desk.

"Good evening," he greeted the woman, emphasizing his poor English. "I'm told a man might find some companionship here!"

"I don't know about companionship but we got girls to screw for money," the woman responded in her crude manner.

"How much?"

"What do you want? We got some young ones, some pretty ones and some average ones."

"How does one pick?"

"You don't, unless you want to spend big. If you got the money, I'll let you look at pictures of them," she said.

"How much?"

"Two hundred."

"Let's see the pictures", he said putting two new hundred-dollar bills on the counter.

The woman plopped a picture album on the counter. Enserro turned it around and opened it up. He went through each page until he found what he wanted on the fourth page. He was careful not to let his face show any emotion when he saw a picture of his niece Tina. He showed her the picture.

"I'll take this one!"

"Fine with me, but that's another hundred."

He started to argue, then put another bill on the counter. The woman grabbed it up, took the picture album back and told him to go down the hallway off to the right of the counter.

He carefully made his way down the dimly lit hallway until he found the way blocked by a man who had to be one of the bouncers. The guy was well over six feet and built like a wrestler. He simply pointed to a door on his left. Enserro opened the door and stepped inside. The room was very small with the only furniture a single, well-worn bed. He went to the window at the end of the room and found steel bars on the inside of the glass. He turned when the door opened, dropped his head so his hat would hide his face from Tina, so she wouldn't cry out his name. When the door was shut, he lifted his head, putting his finger over his mouth.

His niece stood at the end of the bed her eyes open very wide. She wore only a very skimpy top and bikini panties. He pulled her to him, hugging her and telling her he was happy to find her.

"Are you being held a prisoner here?" he whispered.

"Yes," she responded, tears coming to her eyes.

"How long have you been here?"

"Many months. I lost track of time," she said.

"Who brought you here?"

"A very bad Gringo. His name is Bradley Porter."

"How many girls beside you are here?"

"Twenty."

"How many men are guarding you?"

"Only three tonight. There are more on busy nights."

"How long are you allowed to stay with me for three hundred?"

"Thirty minutes!"

"I don't think it will be long enough. Can I buy more time?"

"You can try when the thirty minutes is up."

Enserro took a small cellular phone from his pocket and punched in a number.

Sheriff Jerico Magee was sitting in the large family room at the ranch when the phone on the stand beside him rang.

"Listen carefully sheriff, I won't have time to repeat this. Remember the man in the next cell to Eldon Jones," Enserro said.

"Yes."

"I'm in an old bunkhouse one mile north and a half mile east of the town of Boone. This bunkhouse has twenty young Mexican woman being held prisoner for the purpose of prostitution. I am in a room with my niece who I have been looking for. They think I am a paying customer. I have about twenty-five minutes left. How soon can you send me some help?"

"Hold on, I'll use the other line and call our dispatcher," he said. He put Enserro on hold, dialed the dispatcher and asked who was out on patrol and where they were. He came right back on the line. "I've got three cars out, two of them are on the way. It will take me thirty minutes, can you stall?"

"I'll try. Hurry sheriff," Enserro said then hung up.

Magee grabbed his coat and went out the door on the run. He was in the car and on the highway when he dialed the dispatcher on his mobile phone.

"Where do you show Penny?" he asked the dispatcher.

"She's at home," the dispatcher responded.

"Get her on the phone. Tell her we're on our way to raid an illegal house of prostitution. We need her and some more deputies as soon as they can move. Then get on the radio and see if any state patrolmen are in position to respond and help," the sheriff told her. He was running over eighty when he came to the city limits and started looking for the turn off for highway 50.

In the dispatcher's office, Deputy Sheriff Everett Cline walked through the door. He heard the woman talking on the radio to the state patrol.

"What's going on?" he asked her.

"The sheriff's on his way to raid a whore house north of Boone and he's asking for all kinds of help, Booker's on her way and calling for all available deputies. You better get out there," she said.

"On my way," he said as he left the room. He stopped in the squad room and picked up the phone. He punched in the number of the bunkhouse and swore when he got a busy signal. He waited a few seconds and tried again. This time it rang. The heavyset woman working the counter at the Boone ranch answered.

"There's a shit pot full of cops on the way out there. Someone inside blew the whistle. You ain't got long to get out of there," Cline said then slammed down the phone.

Not five minutes prior to the call, the bouncer had knocked on the door of the small room where Tina Enserro was supposed to be servicing her client. The bouncer yelled through the door that her time was up. Her uncle told her to get on the bed. He pulled open his shirt, mussed up his hair and opened the door a crack.

"This one is so nice, I would like more time," he told the bouncer.

"You got another two hundred for thirty minutes?" the man growled.

Enserro handed him two more bills and pulled the door shut. He was beginning to get nervous. He pulled his automatic from his belt at the small of his back and checked it. He flipped off the safety and waited.

The bouncer walked back to the front counter and handed the two hundred to the fat lady. She was on the phone and took the money and never got to ask whom it was from.

"That was Cline. He said the cops are about to raid the place. Tell the others to get out," she said.

"What about the girls?" the bouncer asked.

"To hell with the girls. You want to spend the rest of the night in jail?"

The woman ran down the hallway as fast as she could move, heading for the back door and her Chrysler in the back lot. As she opened the door, she saw a sheriff's cruiser coming around the building, red lights flashing. She slammed the door and started back up the hallway toward the front. She was last in line behind the three men working security this night. As they burst out the front door, another sheriff's cruiser came across the front parking lot, wheels sliding on the icy surface as the driver was trying to stop. The headlights of the cruiser caught the men as they came out the door. Deputy Sheriff Jimmy Red Bear was out of the car and down on his knees behind the door.

"Sheriff's officer," he yelled. "Stay where you are!"

The first guy out the door pulled an automatic and started firing. The bullets hitting Red Bear's cruiser shocked him at first, and then he aimed and returned the fire. The man shooting, yelled, grabbed his throat and went down. The two behind him spread out, one diving behind another car, the other trying to get around the corner of the building. The fat lady slammed the front door and ran back inside the building. Two highway patrol cruisers came into the front lot, red lights flashing. When the cars stopped, both troopers came out, much the same way Red Bear did.

"There's three of them," he yelled. "One down by the front door. One is off to the left and one ran around the building. All three are armed. Shots fired."

At that second, he heard the second man firing at the state troopers who immediately returned fire.

Jerry Magee turned into the yard in front of the bunkhouse as the second man opened fire. He could see the orange flashes from up near the building and the flashes from the state patrol cars. He slid to a stop and fell out the driver's door, pulling his automatic.

He saw Red Bear leave his cruiser, working his way around the building. He ran across the yard following him. As he cleared the corner of the building, the third man stepped from the shadows and started to fire at Red Bear. Magee aimed with both hands and fired three times. The man fell forward, firing his weapon into the ground. Red Bear reacted by dropping to his knees. All at once it was quiet. Deadly quiet.

"Check him," Magee yelled at Red Bear. "I'm going back around in front." Magee cautiously peered around the corner of the building and saw the state police standing over the second shooter. He stood upright and hurried to the front door. He cautiously opened it, and then turned when he heard someone behind him. It was Penny. She had her automatic in both hands. She nodded at him, and then followed him through the front door. They found the fat lady just sitting on her perch behind the counter like nothing was going on. He told her to come around the counter and into the front room.

She moved slowly, but complied. Magee started down the narrow hallway yelling Enserro's name. The second time he yelled, he heard a response. Michael Enserro came out of a door, an automatic in one hand and his arm around his niece.

"You all right?" he asked Enserro.

"Never better. You made good time getting here," Enserro responded.

"How many in the place?"

"My niece said there were three guards here tonight plus the woman on the front desk," he responded.

"We've got them all then," Magee said relaxing. He put his automatic back in his holster and walked toward Enserro.

"Bring the girl up front. We can watch the woman while the troops search the place."

Chapter 9

1:00 a.m. Sat.
Feb. 5, 2000
The bunkhouse

The deputies Magee saw come through the front door to back up Penny Booker, had been Kevin Reddinger, Freddy Reese and Donny Littig. The three injured in the Jeep wreck. Reddinger and Reese were in civilian clothes. Littig was in uniform. Reddinger and Reese had been home and responded in their own vehicles. Littig was on the way to the station to start his tour of duty and had responded directly to the scene. Magee felt very good about those three. He told Penny to take her men and search the place. He asked Enserro to watch the fat lady and he went outside.

The first security man out the door had been shot in the neck and chest. Red Bear had dropped him. The second man down was wounded in the arm and leg. The state troopers got him. Magee walked around the building to the third man. He was on his back on the frozen ground. He had been hit twice in the chest and once in the head. Red Bear was bending over him. When he noticed Magee he stood up.

"I owe you one for this guy boss. I didn't see him," Red Bear said.

"If he had me in his sights, you would have dropped him," Magee responded.

"Yea. If I could hit him," he said.

"Get on the phone and get the D.A. out here as well as the coroner's office. I'll check with the state boys," Magee said. He went back around front.

"We appreciate the help boys," Magee said to the troopers. "Is there someone you want out here?"

"We better call for a duty sergeant," one of them said.

Magee went back inside and was shocked by what he saw. The small front room was full of scantily clad young women. Many of them were just girls. His deputies were rounding up blankets and putting them around the girl's shoulders.

"We found twenty one. I'll bet some of them are barely thirteen or fourteen," Penny told him. "We couldn't find any regular clothes for them."

"Call in and see if the dispatcher can find us a bus. Have Red Bear transport the prisoner that's wounded to the hospital and if they keep him, arrange a guard. We'll need someone to sit on this place until we're finished with it. Also, when you get time, run down the location of Cline and Dunn. I saw Black's cruiser in back, but I didn't see him anywhere when the excitement was going on. I think it's time we moved on those three. I'm going to send Enserro and his niece on into town," Magee said.

He took Enserro aside and told him to take his niece out to his cruiser and he would meet him there. As they went out the door, the D.A. came in.

"Whenever your dispatcher calls me at this time of night, I figure you always come up with something big. What's this all about?" Walter Sugden asked.

Magee took him outside and showed him the bodies. The coroner's people had arrived and were doing their work. He related the story to Sugden, leaving Enserro's name out of it. He just told the D.A. they got a call from a customer. Sugden stayed another half hour, then left in his car. Magee went to his cruiser and found Enserro and his niece in the front seat, running the heater. He climbed in the back seat and closed the door.

"You are not what you seem," Magee said.

"Sorry about that sheriff," Enserro said, turning around and extending his hand.

"I'm Sergeant Michael Enserro, of the Mexican National Police. I'm up here unofficially. I came looking for my niece Tina. She's my brother's girl. She has been through a very tough time."

"I kind of figured you for something different than what you put on from the first time I saw you in jail. Take my car and go into the station. We'll find your niece some clothes. We need information from you but I'll try to keep you clear of the investigation, officially. You did good here. This place certainly needed to be put out of business. You two go on in now. I'll be along later," Magee said then got out of the car and watched as they drove out of the yard.

It would be daylight before Magee and his people completed their work at the bunkhouse.

Penny saw that the girls were taken to the station, and then called in all the help to interview and process them. She called for immigration people to come down from Denver. She found clothes for all of them and had breakfast brought in. She arranged for hotel rooms for them to stay in until immigration decided what to do with them. She assigned Deputy Reddinger and two women deputies to take care of the girls and guard them. This had all been completed and the girls were in the hotel by ten o'clock when Magee finally made it to the station. He motioned for Penny to come to his office and flopped down behind his desk as she came in. He lit a cigarette and pointed at a chair.

"You are doing one fine job with this, especially with the girls. What about Enserro?" he said.

"We gave his niece some clothes and something to eat. He took her to the hotel where we have the rest of them. He said he would stay with her until immigration tells them they can go back to Mexico. He gave us a good statement on his activities since he came up here. He also gave us a good statement on the night Jones was killed," she responded.

"What about Cline, Black and Dunn?"

"Black responded with Red Bear, but sat in his car in back of the place and did nothing. Cline was on duty and the dispatcher told him what was going on and that he should get out there. Dunn was off duty. The dispatcher said she saw Cline make a phone call after he heard about the raid. It was stupid of him. He momentarily forgot that all incoming and outgoing calls are recorded. I played back the tape. He called the bunkhouse and told them we were coming," she told him.

"Suspend Cline, pending formal charges. Suspend Black too. Send someone to pick up Dixie Flagg and any of her peers you can find. They stay here until they give statements on the protection payments. It's time we put these deputies out of business. Put Red Bear to work gathering up the ladies of the evening," he said.

He was to be greatly surprised at the change of attitude as the day progressed. Dixie Flagg and several of her friends appeared at the sheriff's station on their own accord. Word had spread rapidly about the raid on the bunkhouse. The girls were outraged at those young girls being held prisoner, they came forward to give statements on everything they knew about the crooked deputies. The statements given were so numerous and so damning, the D.A. was called over to the station to approve warrants for the arrest of Cline, Black and Dunn. Penny also convinced a judge to visit the station to sign the warrants. She put Red Bear in charge of arresting the three, but they were too late to find Cline and Black. They arrested Dunn at his home and he was soon in jail. Word of the warrants reached Cline and Black before the judge signed them and they both fled with only the clothes on their backs. All point bulletins were put out on NCIC.

The commercial warehouse district in Pueblo covered several city blocks. It was the center of merchandise storage that was shipped in and out of the state by truck. At the western edge of the district there was a large metal building of recently new construction. It measured over one hundred feet wide by three hundred feet long. There were three large overhead doors on the side facing away from the other buildings. Automatic openers with remote control operated the doors.

There were numerous vehicles coming and going from the building at all hours of the day and with the doors on the side that faced open country, few paid attention to what went on at the building.

Inside the building, in the back corner, there was a loft constructed on stilts that rose up to the ceiling. A long open staircase leads up to the loft. There were two large rooms inside. One was an office; the other was lavishly furnished with couches, easy chairs and a large television set.

Bradley Porter sat in one of the easy chairs, sipping a large glass of bourbon and smoking a cigar. He was watching the local news anchor reporting the sheriff's raid on the illegal house of prostitution on the old Boone ranch. Emphasis was being placed on the slavery part of the story about the thirteen and fourteen year old girls brought to Colorado under false pretenses, then kept prisoner and forced to prostitute themselves with the money going to their keepers. Another story came on about warrants outstanding for two deputy sheriffs. Pictures of Everett Cline and Joe Black were shown as the anchorwoman read off the numerous charges they were wanted for.

The phone sitting on a stand by Bradley Porter's chair rang. He took another sip of his drink, then slowly reached out to pick it up.

"You watching television?" a man's voice asked him.

"Which channel?" Porter said.

"It doesn't make a hell of a lot of difference. It's on all the channels. What about the other two houses?"

"We shut them down last night after the raid."

"What about the girls?"

"They were shipped out west. Our friends in Nevada will use them until things quiet down," Porter responded.

"What about Cline, Black and Dunn?"

"What about them?"

"They will talk. When they find Cline and Black, they will fold and sing like birds. For all we know, Dunn is already talking." the voice said.

"I doubt that, but what are you worried about. They don't even know you exist."

"They have to be silenced. Set it up. I'm not taking a chance on them. Get it ready. Take Dunn out at the first opportunity and when the other two are located, get them. What about the cars? Is that operation safe now?"

"No one has any idea about the shop. It's safe. Stop worrying," Porter said.

"Get those deputies, and shut them up for good," the voice said and the phone went dead.

Porter smiled and slowly placed the phone back on the receiver. He stood up and walked to the window that overlooked the inside of the building. Down below there were over a dozen men working around six new automobiles. They were dismantling the cars to sell off the parts. This was a large "chop shop", referring to the nickname such an operation spawned. Stolen cars from a dozen states were routed here for the purpose that was going on down on the floor of the building. The operation was huge, with millions made each month.

Bradley Porter was a sleaze of the highest order. He was only five feet six inches tall and weighed three hundred pounds. He was a snappy dresser. He wore three hundred dollar suits and loved to have people around him, doing his bidding. He would visit the girls brought up from Mexico and pick out his favorite. She would be brought to the chop shop and locked in the loft for his pleasure until he was tired of her, then she would be sent back and another brought up. He especially liked to break in the virgins, hearing them yell as he caused them pain. He was a poor excuse for a human being. He had no conscious and cared for no one but himself and his pleasures.

He returned to his chair and picked up the phone. When the call was answered he simply said that Cline, Black and Dunn were to be silenced. He put the phone down and took another drink of his bourbon. The individual on the other end of the call returned to cleaning the nine-millimeter automatic lying on the table beside the phone.

Magee was at the office at 6:00 a.m. on Monday. He sat at his desk drinking coffee. He felt very good about all that had been accomplished over the weekend. A slave labor whorehouse had been put out of business and he had enough evidence to put the crooked deputies away for years.

Penny came in at seven and checked in with him. He told her to get some coffee, and then ask Emma to step in too and they would see what was going on. They were settled in his office reviewing the workload when the phone rang.

"I think we ought to transfer Dunn to the state prison in Denver until his trial," the district attorney said.

"That's not necessary Walter. We can keep him safely down here," Magee said.

"Look. You're the one who said that someone got to Eldon Jones. If that's true, they could get to Dunn. I'm signing the order to have him moved. State troopers will pick him up before the days over. No arguments," the D.A. said.

"Your call Walter," Magee said then hung up the phone.

"That's strange," he said.

"What?" Penny asked.

"Sugden is transferring Dunn to the state prison. He doesn't think he will be safe here. I can't figure why he gives a damn either way. Dunn is small potatoes. State troopers are coming after him today. Did he tell us anything after he was booked?" Magee said.

"Nothing. I doubt if they told him much. Cline was apparently the leader. He and Black may know something but we have to catch them first," Penny told him.

"When we're finished here, let's get Dunn in interrogation and have a talk with him. Couldn't hurt to try, if he is about to leave us!" Magee said.

They worked another half hour, and then Emma left with a pile of work to do. Penny went to the cells and took Dunn out and into the interrogation room. Magee joined them, sitting across the table from the prisoner.

"The D.A. called. He's moving you out of here to the state prison. He doesn't think we can keep you safe here," Magee told him. Dunn didn't respond.

"Why would the D.A. be concerned about your safety? Is there someone out there who would want to get to you?" Penny asked him, getting no response.

"You are going away for a long time, Glenn. Your old boss is dead, Cline and Black skipped out and you're sitting here to take the fall for all of them. Did Boone pay you good enough to be the only one to go before a jury?" Magee asked him.

"I suppose Boone gave the orders and you did what you were told, is that about how it was?" Penny asked.

"Boone didn't have much say in anything," Dunn finally spoke.

"You're saying Boone was not the man in charge?" Penny responded.

"I should have a lawyer here," Dunn said.

"We're not going to use anything you say here. We're trying to figure out how to help you stay alive. The way I figure it, someone wants you in the state prison so that they can get to you. Someone doesn't want you or Cline or Black telling what you know," Magee said. "If you have something to contribute, we will get you a lawyer."

"Boone took orders like the rest of us. Our go between was Bradley Porter. I don't know who his boss is. Boone worked hard to kill any investigations into what Porter had going on. The girls out at the old bunkhouse were only one of three places he was running. When you hit the bunkhouse, they closed the other two down. They're running a big chop shop somewhere. I was never privileged to visit that place. I don't know where it is but it's big. Porter was running a shake down on everything in the county. As long as he got a piece of it, the sheriff either protected them or tipped them off when other jurisdictions were getting close. There was always talk about a big warehouse where they ran a fencing operation. It was supposed to be big too," Dunn told them.

"What about Boone's death. Who killed him?" Penny asked.

"I heard enough from Cline talking, to figure the sheriff got to talking too much when he was drinking and chasing the hookers. One of the girls told Cline about Boone shooting his mouth off. They found out Boone was running out of guts and was about to talk. Word is that they have access to a freelance hit man, someone very good. They say Porter hired this hit man to do the sheriff and that black man Jones," Dunn said.

They were interrupted by a knock on the door. Magee stood up and walked across the room. His secretary Emma stood outside.

"There's an attorney out here looking for Dunn. Says he has been retained to defend him. He wants to know why you have him in here without an attorney?" Emma said.

"Show him in," Magee said.

Emma returned in a few moments with a well-dressed elderly gentleman.

"Sheriff, I'm Arthur Nash. I have been appointed to represent Mr. Dunn through his preliminary hearing. Is this an interrogation?" the man asked.

"No Mr. Nash. I would say it is a conversation with Mr. Dunn to figure out the best way to keep him alive until he can get a hearing. The D.A. tells me he is ordering him moved to the state penitentiary. Are you aware of that?" Magee asked.

"I'm not only aware, I requested it. If what happened to Eldon Jones is an example of how safe prisoners are under local jurisdiction, then Mr. Dunn should be in a much safer place," Nash said.

"One difference here Mr. Nash. Jones was being held in the city jail, not here when he was killed," Penny spoke up.

"I insist you discontinue asking my client questions without me being present," Nash said, ignoring Penny's remark.

"Have it your way. Take him back to his cell," Magee told Penny. He got up and left the room as Penny led Dunn out. He was not surprised to find Maddie Patterson sitting in a chair by his secretary's desk. She stood up as he came through the squad room.

"Was Arthur a little rude Jerry?" she asked the sheriff.

"I have been around worse acting attorneys," he responded.

"I think he's just upset that the Judge appointed him to represent the deputy through the preliminary hearing," Maddie said.

"I guess someone has to do it. How is everything going for you?" he asked.

"I'm getting my share of cases to work. Arthur is really a nice person. He treats me civil and is teaching me a lot," she responded.

Emma interrupted to tell him he had a phone call. He excused himself and told Maddie it was good to see her again. He went into his office and picked up the phone.

"I hope I'm not catching you at a bad time," Michael Enserro said.

"Not at all sergeant. Are you back home?"

"Just arrived. My brother put his girl in a hospital for a few days. She may never get over what she went through. If you need any help bringing those responsible to justice, just let me know. I owe them. Your government was most gracious on how they handled returning the other girls. They saw that they all got back to their families. Again, I thank you for your most gracious assistance," Enserro said.

"Your most welcome sergeant. Come see me when you are up this way again," Magee told him, and then hung up.

Penny came into the office and sat down. Magee leaned back in his chair and took a long look at her. The warm feeling spread all over as a fantasy popped into his head. She was talking but he didn't hear her.

"Are you listening?" she said.

"I'm sorry. What did you say?"

"We now have three more vacant deputy spots. Can I start looking for some candidates?"

"Of course. How about lunch?"

"Pardon me!"

"I'm asking you out to lunch."

"Is this a date?"

"Hardly. If it was a date, I would have on my best clothes and we would go out for a nice dinner, then dancing then back to your place where I might chance getting my butt kicked."

"In your dreams! I probably have time for a burger, you buying."

"Let's go," he said as he stood up and grabbed his coat.

They went out the back door just as the state cruiser carrying Dunn and two state troopers pulled out of the lot. Magee watched them go, shaking his head. He followed Penny to her cruiser and climbed in the passenger seat.

The car with the troopers and their prisoner drove to the on ramp of I-25 and headed north. Ten miles north of Pueblo, the cars engine started to miss. The driver spotted a rest area ahead and turned off. No one in the cruiser noticed the dark Dodge minivan as it slowed and followed them down the drive and park near the rest rooms. The trooper was on his radio, calling for assistance. The engine had quit running the minute he stopped at the curb. He ground the starter several times but the engine wouldn't start. The driver of the minivan left the vehicle and went to the rest room building. A few minutes later, one of the troopers took Dunn from the back seat of the car and started toward the rest rooms. He opened the door for Dunn, and then followed him inside. Dunn went to one of the urinals, the trooper stepped up to a mirror beside him, looking at his reflection. They both heard the door of a stall open, then close. The trooper saw a reflection in the mirror that caused his face to change to surprise. The driver of the minivan fired an automatic twice, both shots hitting the trooper in the back. Dunn spun around, his hand still directing the flow of piss. He saw the flash of the automatic as two shots struck him in the chest, knocking him against the wall between the urinals. He slowly slid down the wall, the yellow liquid spreading over his pants and the floor.

The killer took the noise suppresser from the barrel of the automatic, put it in one pocket and the gun in another pocket, and then calmly walked out of the bathroom. The trooper waiting in the disabled cruiser paid no attention as the minivan drove off.

After a few minutes, he got out of the car and went looking for his partner and the prisoner. He opened the door of the bathroom and almost threw up at what he saw. He ran back to the cruiser to use the radio and call for help. Half way through his excited transmission, he had to stop, as he threw up all over the concrete.

Penny and Magee were back in the office after lunch when news of what happened to Dunn and the trooper came in. The dispatcher at the station overheard the traffic on the state radio and gave them the word as they came in. They went back out to Penny's cruiser and headed north on the interstate. When they reached the rest stop, it was crawling with state police vehicles. Penny parked back out of the way and they walked to the rest rooms. They found the officer in charge of the scene who told them what happened. Ten minutes later, the D.A. came driving in. They met him outside the building and didn't say a word as he went by them through the door. He came back out in a few minutes, a sick look on his face.

"I don't want to hear it, Jerry. Someone could have got to him anywhere," the D.A. said. I talked to the state boys. They requested jurisdiction in this one, since they lost one of their own. I told them to go ahead. Stick around until the coroner is finished and help where you can." He then left them before they could say a word, walked back to his car and drove off.

"You can challenge him you know. You have first jurisdiction over a homicide in this county," Penny said.

"I think the state can handle it. I can't figure what's happened to Sugden. He seems to be making a lot of mistakes lately," was Magee's response.

They stayed at the scene another two hours, then left after the bodies had been loaded and the coroner's wagon drove away. Magee was quiet on the ride back to Pueblo as the cruiser sped down the interstate. He was trying to picture in his mind what happened at the rest stop.

"The shooter had to have nerves of steel. The chances were very good that someone might have walked into that toilet and witnessed the killings. Lucky no one did or there would have been more bodies," he said.

"Then to walk calmly out, right by the second trooper sitting in his car. You're right, nerves of steel, a real professional. What did they say about the state car?" Penny asked.

"Simple. They ran out of gas. Someone simply poked a hole in the gas tank, followed them until they stopped, then calmly blew Dunn and the trooper away. They won't soon solve that case," Magee said.

"I should think that Cline and Black better watch their backs, wherever they are," Penny said.

They returned to the office and both soon became busy with the work of the day. A little past seven, Penny stopped by Magee's office and asked him if he could come out to the squad room. He left his chair, following her out of the office. Back in the coffee room, he found Kevin Reddinger, Freddy Reese and Donny Littig.

"Things have been a little busy around here boss, and we never got a chance to tell you thanks for hauling our asses out of the Jeep when it rolled," Reddinger said. "We have noticed a big change around here since you took over and we want you to know we are grateful, not only for the help when we were hurting, but for the way you're running things. We think this will be a good place to work."

Magee turned a little pink at the praise and didn't know what to say. He went to each of them, shaking their hands.

"The feelings are mutual. I think you guys are doing a good job and appreciate your help. Now I'm going to call it a day before you have me all teary eyed," he said, and then walked out. Penny walked with him as he went back to his office. He cleared off his desk, grabbed his coat and walked out the back door. She told him she had some more work to clean up and would see him in the morning. He thought about her and how far they had come in a few days as he drove out to the ranch.

Chapter 10

7:00 p.m. Wed.
Feb. 9, 2000
Las Vegas, Nevada

Everett Cline and Joe Black had been holed up in a room at the Luxor since they fled Colorado. Neither of them had saved much of the money they earned, either from their salary as deputies or the funds from their illegal activities. Las Vegas is a city that requires a lot of money if one stays there very long. What they didn't spend on room rent, food, booze and women, they lost gambling.

Cline called Bradley Porter on Tuesday and asked him to send them some money. He had enough pride not to beg, but told Porter the many reasons they had some big money coming to them. Porter was very reasonable and said they were smart to skip out. They should stay where they were; lay low for a while and he would have more work for them in the future. He promised to send some money.

They had been charging their meals to their room the past two days and thought nothing about who was at the door when they heard someone knock. They were expecting room service with their supper. Black went to the door. When he opened it, he recognized who was standing there.

"What you doing out here?" he said, which were his last words. He never even heard the small popping noise the suppressed automatic made as two bullets hit him in the chest at short range.

Cline came up out of his chair, his hand on the gun in his belt. He had the automatic about half way up when he was hit high in the chest, then twice more as he flew backwards. It was over in seconds. The shooter walked over to him, watched him for a moment, then satisfied that he was finished, turned and walked out of the room, pausing to hang the do not disturb sign on the outside of the door.

County Sheriff Jerico Magee was at his office at 6:00 a.m. on Thursday morning. He found a message on his desk. It was from the Las Vegas police department, telling him that the two men named in his fugitive warrant, had been found murdered in their hotel room in the Luxor. The message continued with a little information about the killings and a personal note that it was the opinion of the investigating officers, that it was a professional hit.

He left his chair and went out for some coffee. He found Penny in the coffee room pouring her a cup. She pulled down another cup and poured him one. He lit a cigarette, sat down at the table and handed her the message as she joined him. She slowly read it, then looked up at him.

"Well that puts us back to square one. We get one step closer to who is behind everything and they put us back two steps. Where do we go now?" she said.

"Dunn gave us the name Bradley Porter. We start finding out everything we can about him and see where that leads. On another matter, there is a statewide sheriff's association convention in Denver next week. Elmer Gray thinks I should attend. I want you to go along. You need to decide who can run things for you when you're gone. Set it up for next week. I'll have Emma handle the paper work and get us some rooms. What's on for today?" he asked.

"I have to be in court at 9:00 and it will probably take all day. Do you know anything about Red Bear and Orville Boone's widow? He did a follow up interview with her and he was complaining about her calling him back out there twice more," she said.

A smile spread over Magee's face. He just looked at her for a minute

"If you're thinking what I think you're thinking, you've got to be dead wrong. Jimmy Red Bear and Eloise Boone. No way," she said.

"Stranger things have happened," he said as he picked up his cup and left the coffee room. He was grinning all the way back to his office.

Magee was busy through the day and it was nearly 7:00 p.m. before he started for the ranch. Charlie Little Crow's wife kept his supper warm for him and made him clean up and sit right down at the kitchen table to eat. He had become very fond of her. He felt very comfortable living in the large old ranch house. He was tired from running all day and was in bed before ten. Toward morning, he woke up with Little Crow shaking him, telling him the dispatcher was on the phone. He picked up the phone by his bed, rubbing his knuckles over his sleepy eyes.

"We have a bad wreck on I-25 just north of the county line. The state patrol is asking for assistance. I sent everyone on duty. They requested four ambulances and the coroner," she told him.

"I'll go take a look," he told her. He got up and started putting on his uniform. He strapped on his gun belt and put on his heavy coat. When he went outside, it was foggy. When he got to the asphalt highway, there was a slick sheen of moisture on the road. He had to hold his speed down and allow extra time to stop. When he reached the interstate, he found the traffic was light and the cars that were out were traveling slowly. It took him, what seemed like a long time, to get to the scene of the wreck. He was close when the flashing red lights on the cruisers suddenly popped out of the thick fog. He slowed and pulled off on the shoulder. He walked over to Jimmy Red Bear standing at the edge of the highway, a flashlight in his hand. He was directing traffic from the north, around the vehicles involved.

"Bad one," he said to Magee. "An old man and his wife ran out of gas. Stopped in the right lane instead of getting off on the shoulder. That van hit the car. No skid marks. Just popped out of the fog on the slick highway and there the car was, in the way. The van rolled.

There were seven in the van. If that wasn't bad enough, a pickup and another car came out of the fog and plowed into the vehicles, sixteen people in four vehicles. Six dead, eight hurt pretty badly and the rest are walking wounded. Good, here's some medical help."

A caravan of ambulances suddenly appeared out of the fog, followed by two more sheriff's cruisers. Magee walked to one of the troopers and asked where he wanted the help.

He worked with his deputies through the rest of the night, loading the injured into ambulances, helping the coroner's people with removal of the dead and getting wreckers out to haul off what was left of the vehicles. Penny had responded with the additional deputies called out. At sunrise the fog seemed to lift and the ice on the highway started to melt. As daylight spread over the scene, there was little evidence left to tell of the deadly scene of just a few hours ago.

Magee was standing by his cruiser when Penny came walking down the shoulder of the highway toward him. He watched her easy gait and how her uniform trousers hugged her legs. That warm feeling again, he thought to himself.

"The troops had complimentary comments about the boss," she said.

"What about?"

"How he gets out and mixes with the working people. Does the same work they do and they like that. It generates respect. They never saw the late sheriff helping."

"It's the only way to be a part of it. Are we done here?"

"The state boys said yes and thank you. They notice the difference too."

"Want to get some breakfast?"

"Meet you at the Country Kitchen on the way in," she commented and started for her car. Magee crawled into his cruiser, buckled up and started the motor. He felt tired. It was going to be a long day. He drove south on the highway until he came to a cross over, then headed north. He pushed the car up to seventy and set the cruise control. He thought about the lifeless bodies he helped the coroner's people pick up and load in their vehicle. It sparked a flash back to Iraq during the brief Gulf War.

He was standing up in a tracked personnel carrier, barreling across the desert at forty miles an hour, when small arms fire erupted off to his right. The enemy was dug in behind a small outcropping of rock along a ridge running a hundred yards across the path of the line of vehicles. He grabbed the fifty caliber on the mount in front of him and began firing. The vehicle bucked up and down, swerving right then left, as he poured fire into the line, like spraying water through a fire hose. When they were very close, the enemy broke and tried to get out of the shallow trench and run. They had nowhere to run. The few that were not cut down by the large bullets, threw up their hands to surrender. When the column finally stopped, there was few left standing.

He couldn't remember getting down from the vehicle, but he clearly remembered walking among the bodies lying in the ditch and behind it, over the sandy terrain. Many of the dead were very young. He walked by three women. When he came to someone alive, he turned and yelled for a medic.

This replay of the dead quit running through his mind as he spotted the exit ahead and the restaurant sitting off to the right. He touched the brake and was soon pulling into the parking lot. He stopped by the front door and went inside. He didn't know how they got ahead of him, but Penny, Red Bear and five more deputies sat at one table with an empty chair for him. He took off his coat and joined them. He felt, for the first time, like he was one of the boys. As he pulled out his chair to sit, Red Bear asked if he was buying, which brought a laugh from all of them. He told them to eat up and it was on him.

They spent an hour eating breakfast, and then everyone went their separate ways, either to finish or start their tour of duty. Magee drove to the office and greeted his secretary as he passed her desk. He was barely in his chair when Red Bear came in the room.

"Got a minute boss?" he asked.

"Any time. Come in."

Red Bear closed the door and pulled a chair over in front of the desk.

"I got a little problem. You know Orville Boone's widow Eloise?"

"Yes. Nice looking woman!"

"She's bothering me. Won't leave me alone."

"Oh! How's that?"

"She's screwing my brains out. I know. I shouldn't get involved with someone in a case but it sort of got out of hand. I went out there to do the follow up interview and before I knew what was happening, she had her clothes off and I couldn't resist. She's got to be a nymphomaniac. She can't seem to get enough."

"What's the problem?"

"It doesn't seem right. She's forty-seven. Twelve years older than me. She just lost her husband and for all I know she could still be a suspect in his murder."

"She seems very attractive."

"Oh she is. She's beautiful. She can get it on time after time. I sometimes have a hard time keeping up with her."

"Do you like being with her?"

"Oh yes. She makes me forget everything but screwing her."

"Where do you think this relationship might go?"

"I have no idea. It may be just good sex."

"Well, I don't see the problem. You are both adults. I don't have her very high on my list of suspects. She is alone and in need of comfort. If you choose to comfort her at this time, I don't consider it a conflict with your duties. You are free to decide."

"Thank you boss. I feel better about it," Red Bear said as he stood up, opened the door and left the office.

Magee watched him go, a broad grin on his face. You're a good man, Red Bear, he said to himself. Penny came in before he let the grin fade.

"Red Bear was spilling his guts about the Boone widow!" she said.

"Well now why would you think that?"

"By the shit-eating grin on your face. You're just tickled that he's getting so much."

"I should be getting half as much!"

"In you're dreams. I'm going home and get some sleep. I didn't get two hours last night. I'll check in this evening," she said.

"I'm going to do the same. I'll be at the ranch if anything comes up. Emma has us booked into the Marriott Sunday evening. The meetings start at nine Monday morning. I'll drive. Pick you up about 3:00 Sunday afternoon," he said. She just nodded and left the office. He told Emma he was going home to catch up on his sleep and walked out of the building.

Chapter 11

10:00 a.m. Sat.
Feb. 12, 2000
Pueblo County Sheriff's Office

Magee had slept late, and then drove in to the office after a leisurely breakfast. The station was quiet, with only the dispatcher and one deputy working in the building. The cells were empty for a change, and the usual deputy on guard was off for the day.

He sat down at his desk and looked through the folders in the basket on his desk. He had not planned to spend much time in the office, but got busy with the reports and it was past noon when he noticed the time. He was about to leave when Maddie Patterson came walking into his office. She was stunning. She wore a light green jacket and matching skirt. Her blouse was cut low, exposing enough of her full breasts to make his mouth water. He was surprised to see her so dressed up on a weekend and even more surprised to find her in his office.

"I called out to the ranch and was told I might find you here," she said.

"What brings you down here on a Saturday?" he responded.

"One of your deputies picked up a client of mine, Joey Sanchez. The charge is grand theft auto. I wanted to discuss this with you to decide whether to advise him to plead or fight it," she said.

"The name doesn't ring a bell. Sit down. I'll find the file," he said. He watched her move to the chair as he stood up and went out to Emma's desk. Her skirt was knee high and showed a large part of smooth thighs as she sat down and crossed her legs.

He brought the file back and opened it on his desk. He briefly looked through it.

"He was caught driving a new Lincoln, which was reported stolen in Denver. He was booked and made bail two hours later," he said.

"He tells me he boosted it to go joy riding," she responded.

"He was picked up on the interstate just north of the city limits. He gave the state patrol and the deputy quite a chase before they ran him off the road," he said.

"What did he say to the officers when they arrested them?"

"Nothing. Not a word. Just wanted to make a phone call to arrange bail."

"What about being in trouble before?"

"Long rap sheet, mostly juvenile offenses. He's now twenty one and can't hide behind the kid status."

"The D.A. really intends to try him for grand theft auto."

"That's what it says," he responded, handing her the file. She took a few minutes to look through the paper work, then handed it across the desk.

"Well he is telling his attorney a different story. I'll have to talk with Arthur and decide what we do with him," she said.

"What was Arthur's response to Dunn getting killed at the rest stop?" he asked.

"It sounds horrible, but I think he was relieved that he was out of it. He abhors representing criminals like him. He's compassionate enough to know that even the worst are entitled to an attorney to see that they are treated fairly under the law, but he argues with the judge every time he has to be the public defender," she said.

"Does that happen often?"

"The judges spread it around to two dozen attorneys if the defendant can't afford legal representation. None of them are very happy when they get appointed."

"Well, I think this Joey Sanchez is going to take a trip on this one, no matter how you plead him," he said.

"You still owe me a meal," she said as she stood up to go.

"I kind of had the idea you and the D.A. had something going!"

"That is strictly court business. I'm certain Walter would like to make it more, but that's how it is."

He stood up as she moved toward the door and was about to walk around the desk when his phone rang.

"Hang on a minute, I'll walk you out," he said as he picked up the phone.

"There is a Sergeant Patrick Lopez on one for you," the dispatcher told him. He punched the button for line one and identified himself.

"We just fished a body out of the river and ran him through the computer. It showed he was out on bond for a grand theft charge your department booked him for. You got time to come out here and take a look?" the sergeant asked him.

"How did he die?"

"The coroner isn't here yet, but it's pretty obvious. Someone put a bullet in his head," Lopez told him.

He asked the sergeant where he was, and then hung up the phone. He went to the door, grabbing his coat as he went.

"I think the Pueblo police department just pulled your client out of the river. You want to go along?" he said.

A look of surprise came over her face but she managed to say she would go along. He took her outside and opened the door of his cruiser for her to get in. He went around to the driver's side and backed the car around and drove out of the lot and the few blocks to the river. He found Lopez and several other officers at the base of the pilings holding up a bridge over the water. Lopez saw him drive up and walked to meet him. He could see the body lying on the ground, covered with a blanket.

"This is Maddie Patterson, Patrick," he said, introducing them. "She represents the deceased there, that is if he is Joey Sanchez."

"That's the name we found on his identification. You want to take a look?" Lopez asked.

"Sure," Maddie said. She followed him back to where the body lay and watched as Lopez pulled back the blanket.

Sanchez couldn't have been more than twenty-one. He was a good-looking kid when he was alive. His face was bloated from the water. A small black hole was very prominent, just above his left eye. Magee watched Maddie for her reaction to seeing the dead boy. She gave no visible reaction at all.

"That's Joey Sanchez," she said, then turned and walked back toward the car.

"Any idea how long he's been in the water?" Magee asked.

"No idea, but it's been a while. When did he make bail?" Lopez asked.

"Sometime Thursday I think. What are you doing out here. I thought running the desk was your domain?" Magee said.

"Oh, the chief sends me outside to work the streets once in a blue moon. He thinks I may get rusty and forget how to be a real cop," Lopez responded.

"Ask the detectives if I can get a copy of the report when they have it put together?" Magee said.

"Will do. I figured you might be interested in this one. It looks like someone is shutting up several people you're interested in," Lopez said.

"If I could only figure out who that is," Magee said. "Thanks Patrick, I'll be in touch."

He walked back to the car and found Maddie in the front seat. He started the engine and drove back to the station. She never said a word on the short trip.

"I haven't eaten yet, you want to go get something?" he asked her as he parked in the lot.

"Another time Jerry. I seemed to have lost my appetite," she said. She got out and walked to her car, without another word, and drove out of the lot. Magee stood watching her go. She is doing well as an attorney, he thought. The car she was driving was a very expensive Lexus. He pondered over her visit as he returned to his office. She could have talked to the D.A. and found out the information he gave her.

What was she really doing down here this morning, he wondered. The sight of her still touched off animal urges in him but he seemed to have lost interest in pursuing her. He cleared off his desk and told the dispatcher he would be at the ranch the rest of the day. He went to his cruiser, drove south until he came to a Burger King and stopped to pick up a sandwich. He ate it on the drive to the ranch, still puzzling the real reason for a visit from Maddie Patterson.

Sunday turned out to be a real day of rest. He was free from calls all day and was at Penny's home late in the afternoon to pick her up for their trip to Denver. He knocked on the door and when she appeared it was like a fresh breath of spring air blowing in his face. He didn't see her in civilian clothes very much. They certainly showed off her full figure. She wore a pair of slacks, knit top and a jacket that matched the slacks.

"You look very nice," he told her.

"I can still kick your ass," she said smiling at the compliment.

She picked up a heavy winter coat and her suitcase, which he took from her and she locked up, then followed him to the car.

He was dressed in a pair of blue jeans, a button down shirt with a sweater over it and a leather jacket.

"You look good in civvies too," she said as she buckled her seat belt.

The drive to Denver took them over two hours from Penny's place to the parking garage at the hotel they were to stay in. Magee checked them in and as soon as they had their bags up to their room, he was knocking on the connecting door to suggest they go looking for some supper. They chose the restaurant in the hotel and when they were seated, both wished they had changed clothes, as it appeared to be an expensive place. They relaxed after they ordered, as several more guests came in dressed much the same as they were. Magee recognized two more sheriffs he knew. More of the working people, he thought.

"You have taken over very well," Penny told him as they sipped their drinks, waiting for their food.

"I've had very good help," he responded.

"We find a few more as good as we have now and it will be the best run sheriff's department in the state," she said.

"There is only one problem to work out yet," he commented.

"What's that?"

"Us!"

"Is there an us?

"That is what needs to be determined. I find you very attractive. I suppose I have been reluctant to hit on you because I didn't know what it would do to our working relationship."

"That and you have been worried about getting your butt kicked!"

"Well, there's that too." The waiter bringing the food interrupted them. They started eating and the waiter returned to the table.

"Are you Jerico Magee?" the waiter asked him.

"Yes," he responded.

"I have a call for you, sir," the waiter said, handing him a phone.

"This is Magee," he said into the phone.

"I'm sorry to bother you sheriff, this is Michael Enserro. I'm in a little of a bind and need your help," the voice on the phone told him.

"Anything you need sergeant," Magee responded.

"I'm being detained by some city police who don't wish to believe I am who I say I am. I wonder if you could come to the police station and vouch for me?" Enserro asked him.

"Of course. Where are you being held?" Magee asked.

"Las Vegas!"

"Pardon me. You said Las Vegas?"

"Yes. I realize it may be a big imposition, but I really need your help."

"You know where I am?"

"Of course, in the Marriott in Denver. There should be a flight out of there at 9:00 p.m. You could be here well before midnight," he said.

"Give me the location where they are holding you," Magee said, and then hung up the phone.

"You're not going to believe this, but I've got to get a plane to Las Vegas," he told Penny.

"When?"

"Now," he said as he waived the waiter over and asked him about the number for the airport. The waiter took the phone and dialed the number for him. He asked about a flight to Las Vegas and was soon connected to the airline. He booked a flight and gave the phone back to the waiter, along with a twenty-dollar bill.

"You have the schedule of the conference meetings. I'm sorry to dump this on you, but go and represent me. I don't know how long this will take, but if you're finished here before I get back, you go on home and I'll get there later," he said.

"So, let me get this straight. You're flying to Las Vegas right now. Who was that on the phone?" she said.

"Oh, I'm sorry. It was Sergeant Michael Enserro. I've learned, when he calls, that it is always something very important," he responded.

"Do you want me to drive you to the airport?"

"No, I'll get a cab. You settle in for the night. The first meeting is at nine. I'll see you when I get back," he said.

He paid for the meal and Penny rode up in the elevator with him. He went to his room and had his bag ready to go in a few minutes. He was putting on his coat, when she opened the door between the rooms.

"You will have a little trouble getting through the airport security with your automatic. Do you have your identification card?" she asked.

He pulled his folding ID case, opened it to show her his card with his picture on it and his badge facing it. He put it back in his jacket pocket, picked up the bag and kissed her quickly on the lips, then left the room before she could respond. She smiled at him as the door closed behind him.

He picked the first cab in line on the street and told the driver he needed to get to the airport. He was dropped at the airline he wanted and went to the desk. He winced at what it cost for the flight on such short notice. He only booked a flight one way, not knowing how long he could be there. He checked his bag and went looking for the boarding gate. Penny was correct about security. He showed his identification and went through quite a lengthy discussion before he was allowed on with his weapon. His identity was verified in their computer and he was on his way.

He boarded the plane shortly after getting to the gate. The flight was not very crowded this late on a Saturday night. Enserro had been correct about the flying time. He was in Las Vegas looking for his luggage at the airport before midnight. His first surprise of the trip was when he found Enserro standing at the bag pickup area waiting for him.

"I see you made the flight, sheriff," Enserro commented as he shook his hand.

"This is a little awkward sergeant, but didn't you say you were being held by the local cops and needed me to vouch for you?" Magee asked him.

"I apologize for the charade. I was concerned about someone listening in on our phone conversation?" Enserro responded. "Let's get your bag, and I will explain in the car."

Magee's bag came up on the turnstile and he grabbed it, and then followed Enserro out of the terminal. They went to a rented Mercury, where he tossed the bag in the back seat and crawled up front with the sergeant. He was soon driving them out of the terminal.

"This trip is a bit more official. That is my government has cleared it with your government. They know I am working here and to some extent have allowed me to work out here alone.

When I returned to Mexico with the girls you helped free, my department interviewed each of them. We found that there were two other locations operating much the same as the one at the old Boone ranch. Both of the places were just over the line in neighboring counties. They closed them down that night and shipped the girls out here. I talked my superiors into letting me continue the investigation and I have located them. I know this is a bother for you, taking you away from you're convention, but I trust you to help me convince the local authorities and help get a raid on the place organized," Enserro told him.

"Where are they?" Magee asked.

"They're being held at a large ranch just off I-15 north and east of the city. It is located near the Las Vegas dunes recreation area, just south of the Moapa River Indian Reservation. I believe prostitution is still legal in Nevada, but slavery isn't. The problem we have is that the ranch is operated by what you call organized crime in this country. Or should I say the mob. I have no idea how much the local authorities are involved. There must be some connection for the mob to operate without being closed down," Enserro said.

"How did you find the place?" Magee asked.

"We have quite a network of informants all over the southwestern United States. With all our people coming and going up here, we have a strong interest to know what is going on."

"We still have to come up with enough evidence to convince a judge to give us a warrant to raid the place," Magee said.

"That's where you come in," Enserro said.

Magee noticed that he turned onto the ramp leading north on Interstate 15. In a little over an hour, they left the interstate and were soon driving down a dusty county road. Twenty minutes later, Enserro slowed for a narrow drive and turned into a clearing with a small house and a barn.

Enserro stopped by the house and shut off the car lights. As they left the car, a man stepped out of the house, a rifle in his hands. Enserro spoke to him, and the man lowered the rifle.

"This is Emanuel," he told Magee, introducing the elderly Mexican. The man gave no indication he wanted to shake Magee's hand. He turned and led them back into the small house.

"Emanuel has some old clothes which will help us pass for locals here," Enserro said.

He and Magee took off their clothes and put on the pants, shirts, coats and hats the man handed them. Magee followed them outside where he saw three horses in a small corral. They were saddled and waiting for them.

"I hope you can ride?" he said to Magee.

"I've been on a horse a few times," he responded, not telling them it was just the few times, Little Crow had taken him out riding at the ranch. The horse he was given was gentle and gave no indication he would be any trouble. They were soon following Emanuel over the dry, dusty ground in the dark. Enserro rode beside him.

"We're going to the ranch?" Magee asked.

"Yes, it isn't far," Enserro responded.

"For what purpose?"

"We are going to take one of the girls out of the place. With her statement and you, telling a judge what you saw, we should be able to get a warrant," Enserro said.

"How much time do we have before daylight?"

"Enough!"

Emanuel reined in his horse ahead of them and dismounted. He tied the horse to a scrub tree, and then disappeared in the dark as Enserro and Magee crawled off of their horses.

"Where did he go?" Magee asked about Emanuel.

"To get us one of the girls. Can you see the ranch house?" Enserro asked.

Magee looked around in the dark, but could see no farther than a few feet.

"We're on a small ridge, look down and to your left," he told Magee.

He could barely make out the large building some seventy-five yards away. Christ, we're awfully close, he thought. This became apparent when they heard someone walking off to their right. Enserro dropped down to the ground but Magee was too late. A man suddenly appeared out of the darkness. For the brief instant before the man saw them, Magee noted he was dressed in military pants and jacket and was carrying a rifle. He was just three feet from Magee when he saw them and started to bring the rifle up. Magee moved quickly, striking the man twice in the head. The man fell like a stone being dropped. Enserro stood up and moved to him.

"Is he dead?" he asked Magee

"No, but he'll have one big headache when he wakes up. What do we do with him?" Magee asked.

"Wait for Emanuel, then take him with us. It might be some time before we come back. We don't want his friends finding him. I'm surprised they have perimeter guards out."

He was interrupted by Emanuel coming toward them hanging onto a small girl. He held his hand over the girl's mouth and led her with his other hand around her arm. She was wearing Emanuel's well-worn jacket, as she had little on underneath it.

Enserro quickly moved to them and spoke to the girl in Spanish. As he talked, Magee could see the fright on the girl's face vanish. She relaxed enough for Emanuel to release her. The girl quietly talked with Enserro.

"This is the place," he told Magee. "She says they were brought here from Colorado in a bus. There are over thirty, not much older than her. She says there have been no customers since they got here but there are at least ten guarding them. Let's get her out of here."

Emanuel helped him drag the guard to the horses. They picked him up and threw him face down across the horse, behind the saddle. They helped the girl up on Enserro's horse, then mounted and started back to the house. The trip back seemed to take much less time than the ride out.

The sun was just trying to climb over the horizon as they dismounted at the house. Magee helped the girl down then helped Emanuel carry the unconscious guard into the house. He was tying the man up as Magee went back outside. He followed Enserro to the car and climbed in back as the girl was put in the front seat.

Enserro started the car and headed back for the city. He picked up a cellular phone and was talking to someone in Spanish. When they reached the outskirts of Las Vegas, he turned off the interstate and drove to a residential area and slowed as he drove down the street, looking for an address. He stopped in front of a large ranch style house, parked at the curb, then leaving the girl and Magee in the car, went up to the front door of the house. Magee saw him knock, and then a man appeared and followed him to the car. Magee slid over in the back seat and the man got in with him. Enserro went around to the driver's side and got in behind the wheel.

"Sheriff, this is District Judge Walter Weston. Your government forewarned him that we would be contacting him. Could you please tell the judge about the raid on the old Boone ranch and what you know about the girls out here? Judge this is Sheriff Jerico Magee, from Pueblo County, Colorado."

Magee shook hands with the judge, and then proceeded to tell him about the girls from Mexico. When he finished, Enserro asked the girl to tell about her captivity. He started to interpret for the girl, but the judge interrupted and said he spoke Spanish. The judge talked with the girl a few minutes, and then told Enserro how to get to his office. They drove to the courthouse and everyone followed the judge up in the elevator. The judge made a phone call then went to a coffee pot and made coffee. A matronly looking woman soon came to work and set up to take dictation. The judge got a written statement from the girl, Magee and Enserro than issued a warrant to raid the ranch house.

"Who can be trusted to do the job?" Enserro asked the judge. He thought that over for a minute, then picked up the phone. He spoke to someone for a few minutes, then put the phone down and dialed another number. He repeated the conversation, and then hung up.

"The chief deputy sheriff can be trusted. I told him to come down here with half a dozen men he could trust. I also told him not to tell the sheriff what he was doing. I also summoned a captain of the state police. We should have a big enough raiding party in a few minutes," the judge said. He poured them coffee, then sat down at his desk and opened a drawer and pulled out a 9mm automatic. He checked the clip, jacked a round into the chamber, put on the safety, then put the gun in his belt. Enserro and Magee looked at each other, as if to say, the judge is evidently going along on this raid.

It wasn't long before the offices filled up with deputies and state troopers. The judge introduced Enserro and Magee and told them to get in their cruisers and follow him. He led them all downstairs and got in the car with Enserro and Magee. The girl had been left in the hands of a bailiff that worked for the judge.

The raiding party made quite a caravan as it barreled down the interstate. When they arrived at the large old ranch house, they surround the building, left the cars on the run and kicked in the doors of the building, yelling police and search warrant as they raided the building.

Inside, they found many young Mexican girls, scared to death. They found none of their guards. Sergeant Enserro asked one of the girls where the men went. She told him that they had all left not five minutes ago in several cars. The judge was furious.

"Shit! Shit! Shit," the judge yelled. I don't know how the son of a bitch found out but I'll bet you that no good sheriff tipped them off." The judge stood in the hallway fuming until he managed to bring himself under control.

"We have a sheriff that works for the local organized crime syndicate. I haven't been able to get him yet, but I will. I also suspect our district attorney, which you see I left out of this too," the judge said. "Let's get these girls into town and get statements from them. We'll see if that one you caught will talk. The rest of you search every inch of this place.

You're looking for anything that tells you who owns the place and who was keeping these girls here against their will."

A state correctional bus was summoned and all the girls were taken to the city. The officers spent two hours searching the house but found nothing they could use. Magee and the sergeant took two deputies with them and picked up the guard Emanuel was keeping at the small house. They transported him to the courthouse and the judge met them in a conference room. A scared young attorney was with him. The judge had appointed him to represent the guard while they questioned him.

They spent half an hour with him and found out nothing. With or without the attorney, the man wasn't going to talk.

"Well, I guess it was not all for nothing. We set the girls free and will get them back to their families," the judge said.

Enserro thanked the judge for all his help, then he and Magee left. He drove Magee to the airport and waited while he purchased a ticket back to Denver. It was 2:00 in the afternoon and both were hungry. They found a coffee shop and ordered some lunch.

"I am aware of how much I put you out, but I don't think any of this would have happened without your help," Enserro told him.

"The main thing is the girls are free again. You going right back?" Magee asked.

"I'll stay and go back with the girls. Are you any closer to who is behind all this?"

"We probably are but don't know it. It's just a matter of time, we'll figure it out," Magee said.

Enserro stayed with him until his flight was called, then wished him well. He boarded the plane and found the cabin full. The flight did not seem long and he was soon picking up his bag in the Denver airport. He hired a cab to take him to the Marriott Hotel and was dropped by the front door a little after six. He went up to his room, dropped his bag and went into the bathroom. He looked at his face in the mirror. He was tired. He hadn't been to bed since Saturday night. He stripped down and shaved, then took a long shower.

He dried off with a large towel, pulled on his shorts and crawled into bed. He was soon asleep.

Chief Deputy Penny Booker was finished with the last meeting of the day at 9:00 p.m. She went to her room and opened the door between her room and Magee's to leave the days hand out material on his credenza. She was surprised to find him in bed, snoring like a sawmill. He was lying on his back in his shorts, the blanket loose beside him. She smiled as she appraised his strong muscular chest, flat hairy stomach and the mound of his manhood under the shorts. She had an urge to run her hand under his shorts, but it soon passed. She pulled the blanket over him and went back to her room. She thought about him as she undressed and ran water in the bathtub. He hit the nail on the head when he brought up the subject of them getting together. She could feel their attraction growing each day. She had a warm feeling each time she saw him or was with him. There was definitely a physical attraction. She felt a stirring down deep just thinking about him in the next room in his briefs. She wondered what it would do to their working relationship if she got him into bed. She soaked in the tub until her skin wrinkled, then climbed out and dried off. She stood in front of the long mirror, looking at herself. She wasn't getting any younger. Sure she looked fine now. Firm breasts, smooth stomach, legs just right, everything to attract him. She took a short nightgown from her bag and pulled it over her head. She turned off the overhead light and crawled into bed.

Chapter 12

Tues.
Feb. 15, 2000
Marriott Hotel- Denver

Penny was up and dressed before eight. There was one last meeting in the morning before the convention closed. She dressed for the meeting, and then went to Magee's room. He was sleeping soundly, his breathing slow and even. She stood watching him for a moment, and then went back to her room, then out the door to find some breakfast.

The meeting in the large conference room was planned to share information about crimes across the state that might be common to all jurisdictions. The speaker at the podium was an assistant attorney general. Magee came into the room as the young lady began to speak. He looked around for Penny. He spotted her at about the same time she saw him. She waived for him to come sit in an empty chair near her. He made his way through the many tables and smiled at her as he sat down.

The speaker was talking about the large number of car thefts around the state and in neighboring states. She listed off the many expensive models being stolen and the very few recovered. When she finished, she asked those in attendance to add any information they might have. Several of the participants stood and told about the activities in their jurisdictions.

The meeting ended on schedule and Magee went up to the rooms with Penny to get their bags to check out and start back for Pueblo.

"How did the meetings go?" he asked her.

"They were all good but one on case law. The guy talking about put me to sleep. How did your trip turn out?" she asked.

He filled her in on his quick trip to Las Vegas as they gathered up their clothes and packed. They went downstairs, checked out of the hotel and found the car.

They stopped for lunch at the south edge of the city. Magee had a feeling that he had experienced an opportunity missed. He was in a nice hotel, in a room next to this very attractive woman and he had to run off and spend all the time chasing around the desert in Nevada.

They made it back to Pueblo by late afternoon and Magee parked in the lot at the sheriff's station. They went inside to check on the activities of the past few days. They were busy until after six when Penny stopped by his office to tell him she was taking off and would see him in the morning. He thought about asking her to have supper with him, but was interrupted by a phone call and let it go. He watched her as she left the office, an audible sigh escaping his mouth.

The call was from Virgil Dykes, the pawnbroker. He asked Magee to stop by his store when he had time. Magee told him he would be right over. He dropped his paper work back in the basket on his desk, grabbed his coat and left the office. He drove across town to the run down pawnshop and found Dykes perched on his stool behind the counter. When Dykes saw him come in, he came around the counter, went to the front door and locked it. He led Magee into the back room where he sat down at a desk. Magee pulled up a folding chair and sat down, lit a cigarette and sat staring at Dykes.

"Word has it you been doing a good job as sheriff," Dykes said.

"You didn't call me down here to pat me on the back Virgil," Magee responded.

"I didn't expect you to take the compliment any different. You don't go looking for praise. That's one reason a lot of us lesser privileged want you to succeed. What I got for you is some information I picked up here and there. I don't know nothing personally and I can't testify to what I'm about to tell you," Dykes said.

"Get on with it Virgil," Magee said with impatience.

"Eight or nine years ago, an operation was set up to control all the action around here. It started out with three or four people in positions of authority who controlled their own territories. A new player arrived in town and organized the others and got them to working together. They started to run things like a board of directors in some company. The late Sheriff Orville Boone became a member of the board. They were soon controlling everything. Anyone or anything illegal didn't operate unless a piece of it went to the board. The profits soon came pouring in, millions of dollars. With all the different people involved, it soon became evident that they needed someone to run the operation on a day-to-day basis. That's when Bradley Porter came to the surface. He was put in charge of the processing of the stolen cars, the gambling, loan sharking, and anything else that would make a buck. Porter got hooked up with some bad asses out of Mexico and started bringing in the women from south of the border. They brought them north with the promise of good jobs and a new life. What they got was being locked up and forced to be prostitutes. The members of the board were pissed at first until the money came rolling in. The money always soothes the conscious. The late sheriff couldn't handle using little girls like that. He got to drinking more and more. He spouted off about putting an end to it. He must have told the wrong person and the board soon heard about it. They had him taken out. They have some professional to eliminate anyone that's a problem. The sheriff, Eldon Jones, the three deputies and that kid they caught with the stolen car. They were all silenced.

They put a bomb in your place, but missed. They're not too happy about your activities. You put their whorehouses out of business and they are not too happy about the pressure you're putting on their other operations. Word is they are coming after you again, because you were in on raiding the ranch in Vegas."

"How did you find out about that? It just happened?" Magee asked him.

"The place belonged to the organization. This local board of directors has some connection with the mob. They were just doing a favor for Porter. They weren't too happy about the raid. They figure your next move may be on their car operation," Dykes said.

"Any idea where the chop shop is?"

"No idea. It has to be right here in the city though. It would be too hard to hide out in the open country."

"Any names of the members of this board of directors?"

"No names. There's supposed to be four of them now with Boone gone. They have a lot of juice, whoever they are."

Magee thanked Virgil for the information and returned to his car. Magee was not aware of it but this board of directors was meeting at the same time he was driving out to the county ranch.

The meeting was at the home of the attorney Arthur Nash. Nash was the connection to the mob. He had represented many members of the organized crime families over the years. Nash lived in a large, sprawling two-story house that looked a little out of place in this city of ranch style houses. Nash acted as chairman of the board at the meetings, but was by no means the one with the power.

The group sat around a table in the dining room. Nash's butler and maids were serving their supper. When they finished eating and were sipping their brandy, the meeting began. Nash looked at the men sitting around the table. On his left was Police Chief Daniel Morrison. The next man was Chief of Detectives Lieutenant Aaron Winters and the last man was District Attorney Walter Sugden.

"Our friends in Vegas were a little upset about the raid on their ranch out there. When Porter shipped those girls to them, they figured it was not going to be a problem," Nash said.

"Big deal. So it's the end of using kids for prostitutes. I say we are a lot better off out of that business," Chief Morrison said. "How did they find the place?"

"I don't have all the information yet," Nash responded. "But our new Sheriff Magee was involved somehow. He was there when they hit the place."

"Magee. All we hear anymore is what Magee is doing. This is all you're fault Winters for hiring the guy and bringing him here. Then our district attorney gets the bright idea to get him the sheriff's job. Would you like to explain that Walter?" the chief said.

"I will admit I underestimated Magee," the D.A. said. "I thought he would be less of a threat in the county office than he was poking around in your department. In any case, Magee has to go. He will ruin everything we have worked very hard to set up. I'll see that he is taken care of. Now let's get on with the meeting. What were the receipts for last month?"

The meeting broke up by nine and everyone left. The D.A. drove across the city to his apartment. He put his coat in the closet, fixed a drink and picked up the phone. When the call was answered on the other end, he simply said it was time for Magee to be eliminated. He put the phone down and thought back to the missed opportunity when Magee escaped the explosion. "You will not be as lucky this time, Jerry," he said out loud.

At the ranch south of the city, Magee had enjoyed a fine meal Little Crow's wife fixed for their supper. He sat in the large front room watching a movie with them. He went to bed at ten thirty with no idea he would not get a good nights sleep.

A few minutes past midnight, the phone beside his bed rang. He was groggy as he searched for it.

"We have an officer down," he heard Penny's voice say.

"Who?"

"Lavern Johnson. He took a disturbance call at that roadhouse out by Lime. He tried to stop a fight in the parking lot before backup arrived."

"How bad is he?"

"Shotgun in the chest. Not good. He's on the way to the hospital by ambulance."

"Where are you?"

"I'm just about to the off ramp on I-25."

"You have some help?"

"Two cars are there and one behind me."

"I'll be there in a few minutes," he responded and hung up.

He dressed in a hurry, checked his automatic and went outside to his cruiser. The engine roared as he pushed the accelerator to the floor. It took him fifteen minutes to reach the run down tavern sitting out in the country. He found Penny and the other deputies in the parking lot, interviewing the few patrons of the tavern.

"This place is the watering hole for every bad ass in three counties," Penny said to him as he left the car.

"Three men, all brothers, got into an argument inside with a big guy named Jed Wilson. The three are Lenny, Seth and Randal Weams. They ganged up on this Wilson and drug him out here to the parking lot. When Johnson got here he found the Weams brothers beating Wilson with a club. Johnson managed to get Wilson away from them, and then Randal Weams went to his pickup and came back with a pump shotgun. He just blasted Johnson, got in the pickup with his brothers and left. The backup deputies found both Johnson and Wilson on the ground when they got here. They put them both in an ambulance. They were pulling out when I got here.

"Anyone here know these Weams brothers?"

"The bartender, but he isn't talking?"

"Is Red Bear here?"

"He's inside."

Penny led Magee inside the building. The place was so dimly lit, they had to pause a moment for their eyes to adjust to the light. A tall, thin man wearing a soiled white apron stood behind the bar. Red Bear was sitting on a stool, talking to the man.

"This guy co-operating?" Magee asked Red Bear, sitting down on a stool beside him.

"No, he says he didn't see a thing, boss," Red Bear responded.

"Who called it in?"

"One of the customers. It was all over, with Johnson and this Wilson down and bleeding in the parking lot, before they bothered. None of them will admit to being the one that called though," Red Bear said.

"You got your skinning knife with you?" Magee asked him.

"Right here," Red Bear said, pulling a long hunting knife from his boot.

"Take this guy back in the bathroom and cut off one of his ears. Maybe that will help his memory," Magee said.

The man behind the bar showed no response to Magee's statement until Red Bear got off the stool and started down the bar and around behind. As he approached the bartender, the man responded.

"You can't get away with that bull shit. I got my rights."

"To hell with your rights!" Magee said. "If one ear doesn't convince him, take the other one too. One of your low life customers shot my deputy. You think I give a damn how much Red Bear cuts you up."

Red Bear grabbed the man by the throat with his left hand, bringing the knife up into his face where he could see it.

"You want me to do it right here boss, or back in the can with no witnesses?" Red Bear asked.

"Take him back there. I don't give a damn who sees it, I just don't want to hear him scream," Magee said.

Red Bear started down the bar, his chokehold tightening around the bartender's throat, the man could barely speak.

"All right. Okay. It was those Weams boys. They always raise hell when they come in here," the bartender said. Red Bear released his throat as he began to talk.

"They came in here around eight and sat at a table drinking. They had some beef with this Wilson, cause when he came through the door, they started picking on him.

He was a big guy but no way he could handle all three of them. Those Weams are mean. They're no good," the bartender said.

"Where do they live?" Red Bear asked him.

"They got a cabin over by Beulah. Sets back in the woods," he responded.

"Take this guy to the station and get a full statement," he told Red Bear. "Do we have anything on what they're driving?"

"We called it in along with their description. It's on the air by now," Penny told him. She stopped talking as they heard yelling from out in front of the building. They went to the front door and out to the parking lot. A group of five men were arguing with two of the deputies and shoving them around. One of the deputies lost his balance and was knocked to the ground. Neither Penny or Red Bear were aware of how fast Magee moved across the parking lot, until they saw him grab one of the men, throwing him to the ground. This sparked the others to turn on Magee, which was a mistake. Jerico Magee had been well trained in about every martial art method of hand to hand combat there is. The first man went down from a blow to the solar plexus then another to the side of his head. The next man screamed as his arm was broken. The third man was kicked in the mouth, then had his legs swept out from under him. The last two were sober enough to see they were outmatched. They backed off, holding their hands out in front to indicate they didn't want any of what Magee was putting out. As soon as it started, it was over. Penny and Red Bear just stood staring, amazed at how quickly the fight was taken out of the group. Magee helped the deputy up and told him to haul all five of the men in and book them and to take anyone else along that gave them any trouble. The parking lot was soon cleared of all the customers. Magee walked back to Penny and Red Bear. He appeared very calm.

"Get a judge out of bed and get a warrant for all three of the Weams brothers," Magee told them. "Lets see if that bartender can give us some precise directions to that cabin?" he continued as he walked toward the tavern.

The bartender was more than willing to tell them anything they wanted to know.

"What are the chances they went to their place?" Penny asked.

"Well, it's the first place to look," Magee said. "Leave a couple deputies here to finish up. We'll take the rest with us. Send this guy in with the five outside. Red Bear, you come along with us."

Penny and Red Bear climbed into the cruiser with Magee. Deputies in two other cruisers followed them as they drove back to the interstate and headed south. They turned off on the road to San Isabel and before they came to the small town, turned north on the road to Beulah. When they reached this small community, they drove on through. The town sat along the east edge of the mountains. As they headed north, the road became a narrow rock trail winding around the foothills. It took them an hour to find the driveway that led off the road back into the wooded area. They passed it twice and backtracked. Magee turned the car onto the drive, which was nothing more than a trail, a very rough trail. Three quarters of a mile further on they came out into a clearing with a small, rundown cabin sitting among the trees. Magee parked at the edge of the clearing, shut off the engine and sat looking the site over. A black, beat up old pickup sat in front of the building. No one was in sight. He left the car as the deputies came up behind him. He gave instructions to surround the cabin and waited as the men worked their way around the clearing to the back of the house.

Red Bear and Penny were standing beside Magee when he started walking toward the front door. He was halfway across the clearing when he shouted.

"Hello the cabin! This is the sheriff! Who's in there?"

He waited for a response, and then resumed walking.

"This is the sheriff. Is anyone in the cabin?" he yelled again. No response. He walked up to the front door, raised his foot up and kicked it open. He pulled his automatic from the holster and walked through the door. There was one room in the small building with a loft built up against the back wall. A short ladder led up to the loft. Red Bear and Penny came through the door behind him. He motioned for Red Bear to check the loft.

Red Bear was half way up the ladder when they heard him speak.

"Get up out of there," Red Bear said to one of the brothers hiding under some blankets. The young man slowly stood up, his hands in the air. Red Bear backed down the ladder and motioned for the man to come down. When he was on the floor of the cabin, Red Bear grabbed him and handcuffed his hands behind his back.

"What's your name?" Penny asked.

"Seth Weams," he said.

"Where's Lenny and Randal?" Red Bear asked.

"They took off when they heard you coming."

"Took off. How, on foot?" Magee said.

"That old pickup is all we got. They took off out the back and made for the hills," Seth said.

"They got the shotgun with them?" Penny asked.

"Randy had the shotgun. Lenny took his rifle," the young man told them. "Randy should never have shot that cop. Lenny and I told him there was hell to pay for that."

"Send this one in with two of the men. What's the ground like west of here? Can we use the horses to go after them?" Magee asked.

"It's too steep and rocky for horses. We'll have to go after them on foot. There's a fair road five miles on west. We could send some men around to block them off if they get that far," Red Bear told him.

"Send the other car around then. Who's going with me?" Magee asked.

"We should have some water and food before we take off up those slopes," Red Bear said. You and Penny start out. I'll gather up some supplies and get a couple more deputies to come along. We'll catch up with you."

Magee and Penny found a path in back of the cabin. It led off through the trees toward the high rocks to the north. Penny went to the cruiser and took a rifle from the trunk. The morning was overcast with the sun trying to peak through the clouds. Magee took stock of what he had on. He wore a heavy uniform jacket and had a pair of leather gloves in one pocket. He took two extra clips for his automatic from the glove box. He also traded his wide brimmed hat for a ball cap.

"You warm enough in that jacket?" he asked Penny.

"It will probably be too warm after hiking for a mile or two," she responded. "Let's go!"

They went around behind the cabin and started up the trail. The only discomfort he felt was his stomach growling. He wished he had some coffee and breakfast. The narrow path twisted around through the dense growth of trees, getting steeper as they walked along.

"They have the advantage of knowing the lay of the country ahead," Penny told him as a warning since he was in the lead. She was concerned that they could wait up high ahead of them and pick them off with the rifle. She followed along, watching where she placed her feet on the rocky ground. The trail rose steadily upward for half an hour as they climbed, then crested out on a ridge. They came out of the trees and could see for some distance. A half-mile ahead, the base of a mountain was thick with pine trees. A valley led off to the left between two mountains. The ground ahead of them was open for several hundred yards, and then a forest of trees grew up both sides of the valley. They could still make out the trail as they started down from the ridge. When they reached the end of the clearing, they could not make out a path any more. It just stopped. The trees were very thick. The valley floor was covered with pine needles and brown grass. Magee stopped by a group of rocks and sat down, fishing a cigarette from his pocket. He found his lighter and sat looking at the ground ahead of them.

"Would they go through the valley or start up the slope to the right?" he asked Penny.

"I don't know them but from what we saw in the cabin, I would say they are lazy. They would take the valley instead of the slope. They eventually will have no choice, but for now, I pick the easier route," she said.

She walked into the forest a short distance and bent down looking at the ground. She pointed and Magee came up to her. She was pointing at the imprint of a boot in the wet grass. Magee nodded and started off again.

They kept up a steady pace well past noon. They would stop for brief rest periods, and then continue on. The sun burned through the low clouds and both were sweating under their heavy jackets.

They came to a creek flowing down the slope toward the direction they came. The water looked crystal clear. Magee scooped some up in his hand and tasted it. Satisfied it was clean enough to drink, he filled both hands and quenched his thirst. Penny squatted down beside him, doing the same. Feeling refreshed again, they started off, walking along the creek bed.

After climbing another hour, Magee suggested they sit down to rest and let Red Bear catch up. Penny didn't argue as the hike was wearing her out. She sat down on the rocky ground, leaning against a large pine tree. Magee sat down beside her on an outcropping of rock. They didn't hear Red Bear when he caught up. The first they knew he was near was when he spoke to them from a few feet away.

"You two covered a lot of ground for amateurs," he said. He was walking along the creek bed behind Charlie Little Crow.

"I called for someone who was good at tracking," he said. Little Crow greeted them, and then walked on by continuing up the creek bed.

Red Bear had a backpack, which he took off. He opened it up and handed out sandwiches and coffee to both of them. Magee was surprised to find the coffee still hot. When they finished eating, they followed Red Bear as he took off after Charlie Little Crow.

Penny and Magee followed Red Bear at a pretty fast pace for half an hour until they could see Little Crow ahead. They were covering less ground, as the climb was getting steeper. They would walk through thick growths of trees, then out in the open over rough, rocky stretches of ground. Little Crow stopped ahead and waited for them to catch up.

"They have been watching us for some time. They split up ahead and have an ambush set. Look up to the left a hundred yards, by that big rock. One of them is down by that tree. The other is off to the right twenty yards, on that flat ground with rocks just below. They expect us to come up between them," Little Crow told them.

"Can you flank them on the right?" Magee asked him.

"Easy. Red Bear can do the same on the left. You going up the middle?" Little Crow asked.

"It won't be a big deal if you two are in place. What's the range on their rifle?" Magee asked.

"I don't know what they have, but they should be able to pick you off when they can see you right now," Little Crow responded.

"What's the range on Penny's AR 16?" Magee asked.

"She will have to be closer than this," Red Bear said.

"You two go ahead. We'll go up the center. About half way there, Penny will set up to cover me with her rifle. The first shot from either one of them, everybody let them have it," Magee said.

Both deputies started moving, using what cover they could. Penny started to say something to Magee but he interrupted her.

"I don't expect either one of them are good shots with a rifle," he said. "Let's go!"

He stepped out into the open and started climbing again. She fell in behind him, holding the rifle in a position to fire in a hurry. They struggled up the sharp incline until they were what Magee thought was within fifty yards of where the two brothers were hiding. He turned to tell Penny to set up a covering position when he heard the sharp report of a rifle. He dropped to the ground at about the same instant a bullet smacked into the trunk of a pine tree behind him and just left of where Penny was. She was soon flat on the ground behind him. Magee aimed his automatic and fired several shots. He could hear Penny open up with the AR-16. He could hear pistol fire from the right and left of the brothers' position.

He could see chips flying from bullets hitting the rocks around both positions. The man on the right yelled something, stood up and threw down his rifle. The man on the left, scurried out of his hiding place and started climbing again as fast as he could. They could see he was carrying the shotgun.

Magee and Penny stood up and started climbing again. Little Crow appeared next to the man who wanted to surrender. When they reached their position, the man had his hands cuffed behind him.

"Which one is this?" Magee asked.

"Say's his name is Lenny. Wants a lawyer," Little Crow said.

"Well, he's going to need one, but I don't think we'll find one out here. Keep an eye on him for a little while. I don't think his brother is going much further. If he gives you any trouble shoot him. Don't kill him just wound him good. I don't want to have to carry him out of here," Magee said. "Did you see where Red Bear went?"

"He's still climbing off to the left. He'll be gaining on the last one. When he gets ahead of him, watch for the last one to turn and come back at you," Little Crow said.

Magee and Penny climbed up the rocky incline, slowly moving over the loose rock and soil, around the short scrub trees and brush and through the shallow cuts in the ground caused by years of rain water rushing down to the creek bed. Little Crow had been right about what Randal Weams would do. Fifty yards ahead, they suddenly heard three shots from an automatic, followed by the boom of a shotgun being fired. Looking up the slope, they saw Red Bear ahead of the third

Weams brother. Randal was coming their way, he would pause, turn toward Red Bear, fire the shotgun, and then stumble down the slope.

Magee picked an open, flat spot to wait for the fugitive. He positioned Penny behind a small tree, and then walked toward Randal who was rushing toward them, not thinking about anything but getting away from Red Bear.

Means was ten feet from Magee when he saw him. He started to bring the shotgun up to fire at the sheriff but was too late. Magee moved to him too fast. As the gun came up, Magee grabbed the barrel with his left hand and pulled. The gun came out of Mean's hands and he fell forward. Magee struck him with his right hand, knocking him to the ground. Means didn't get back up. Penny came up behind him as Red Bear came from the front.

"Is he dead?" Red Bear asked.

"I hope not. I don't want to pack his sorry assed carcass back down," Magee said as he bent over the man and felt for his pulse on his neck.

"No he's just out cold. When he comes around, we'll make him walk back down," Magee rolled him over and put handcuffs on him. He then sat down and lit a cigarette. Penny sat down beside him.

"That was a little foolish," she said.

"What?"

"Walking up on him like that. He could have shot you."

"It wasn't as bad as it looked. His gun was empty."

"You sure?"

"Check it."

Penny picked up the shotgun and worked the action open. The gun was empty.

"It only holds seven shells. He fired seven. I think he's coming around all by himself.

Let's get him back down to his brother," Magee said as he stood up. Red Bear pulled the man to his feet and started him down the slope.

Means whined and complained all the way down. It didn't take long to reach the clearing where Little Crow was sitting watching Lenny Weams.

"They don't look so tough now," Little Crow said.

"They're just three bullies who get their courage from being together or out of a bottle. Separate them and each one loses his courage. Let's get them down to the cabin before it gets dark," Magee said. Little Crow started off in the lead, Lenny behind him. Red Bear put Randal Means out in front of him with Penny and Magee last. The trip down was much easier and they made good time. The sun was setting behind the mountains to the west when they reached the cabin. They put one brother in a cruiser with Red Bear and Little Crow and the other one in with Reddinger and Reese. Penny and Magee sat in Magee's cruiser eating the rest of the lunch from Red Bear's backpack.

"I think I will have to back down a little," Penny said.

"About what?"

"About being able to kick your ass. From what I've seen the past couple days. I'm not so sure I can," she told him.

Magee turned and looked at her, a grin spreading over his face.

"Does that mean I'm now free to try and jump your bones?"

"You wish!"

"If you're finished, let's head for the station. If the troops are getting the paper work started on the Weams brother's, maybe we can go home and get some sleep. I'm bushed," he said.

They were back on I-25 heading north when Penny made a call to the hospital to check on the deputy who was shot in the roadhouse parking lot.

"Johnson is better off than we thought," Penny told him. "He had his vest on. It took most of the shotgun pellets. He was hit in the neck and left arm pretty bad, but will recover."

"That's good news. Does he have any family?"

"Wife and two small kids. The wife has been at the hospital."

"Make sure they get anything they need and see that Johnson takes enough time to get well mentally as well as physically," he told her.

They reached the station by nine and spent an hour checking on the booking process. Each brother was put in a separate cell. Each of them made a phone call for an attorney. The deputy that monitored the calls said that no one was going to show tonight.

Magee left to go to the ranch and Penny left shortly after he did. She was thoroughly exhausted and went to bed ten minutes after she made it to her house.

They both slept in the next morning, but by noon on Thursday were back at the sheriff's station checking on the Weams brother's case. They had been denied bail at their preliminary hearing and the judge had to appoint attorneys to defend them.

Magee was busy through the rest of the week and then was able to get off Saturday. He was at the ranch, sitting out on the big porch drinking coffee and enjoying the warm morning when Little Crow brought him a portable phone.

"Sorry to bother you boss," Red Bear said. "Lenny Weams wants to talk to you."

"What about?"

"He wants to trade information for a deal on his charges."

"Can't he tell you or even better talk to the D.A.?"

"Says he'll only talk to the sheriff."

"I'll be there in a little while," Magee said and handed the phone back to Little Crow. He finished the coffee and went inside to get his gun and jacket. He drove into the city and found Red Bear in the squad room.

"Bring him to the conference room. Does he want his attorney present?"

"Just wants you," Red Bear said. Magee waited until Red Bear brought the man from the cell, then went into the conference room.

Lenny Reams was the youngest of the three brothers. He was over six feet tall and very skinny. Skin and bones Magee thought to himself.

"Got a cigarette?' Lenny asked him.

Magee handed him his pack and lighter. Lenny lit the cigarette and leaned back in his chair.

"I got something that ought a be worth some kind of a deal," Lenny said.

"You know I'm not the one to make any deals. It has to be the D.A.," Magee responded.

"You got more pull than you're lettin on sheriff. I figure a word from you and I don't get as much as brother Randy is going to get. He shot the deputy, I didn't."

"You were there and took part in the beating. You were there when my deputy was shot. You took off, and then shot at my deputies and me. You're looking at a lot of years in the big house Lenny," Magee said.

"I know. I know. Word is there's a contract out on you right now," Lenny said.

"That information isn't worth trading. You mean there's an open contract for anyone that wants to try to get me?" Magee asked.

"No. A pro has been hired to take you out. You must be pissing some big shots off," Lenny said.

"You're wasting my time Lenny. Get to it or I'm leaving," Magee said.

"How about if I give you Brad Porter," Lenny said.

"Now you have my attention."

"My brothers and I pull some jobs for him every once in a while. We boost some expensive cars for him too. I can tell you where his chop shop is," Lenny said.

"Now you're coming up with something worth dealing."

"I can take you there and show you. I can also give you a statement on several of the things we did for Porter," Lenny said.

"Okay, Lenny. I can talk to the D.A. and the judge about a plea bargain knocking the charges down. I'll get a stenographer in here and you start talking. When you're through, we take a little ride and you can point out where Porter takes all the hot cars," Magee said. He left the room and called Red Bear over to stay with Lenny. He went to the dispatcher and asked her to call a stenographer in as well as Chief Deputy Penny Booker.

While he waited, he called the district judge on duty and gave him the information Lenny had. The judge said when he had the statement and information from Lenny he would issue a warrant. He asked why Magee wasn't going through the D.A.'s office. Magee told him he would bring him in on it if they found anything.

Penny came into his office as he hung up the phone. He told her what he had and asked her to organize a raiding party. He went back to the conference room and sat listening to Lenny's testimony. When he was through, Red Bear handcuffed him and took him out to the parking lot, then put him in the back seat of Magee's cruiser. Penny took the passenger seat in front. Red Bear got in back with the prisoner. Lenny directed Magee as he drove across the city to the warehouse district. He showed Magee where to turn as they drove the streets down between the many large buildings. When he pointed out the building where Porter was running the operation, Magee stopped and parked across the street a half block away.

"There ain't a lot going on in there on the week ends. There'll be guys bringing in the new stuff, but the crew taking them apart usually works on week days," Lenny told them.

Magee didn't stay parked long, not wanting attention drawn to the marked cruiser. He drove back to the station and Lenny was taken back to his cell. They went to Magee's office to discuss the raid.

"When's the best time to go?" Magee asked.

"All we have to do is find one stolen car in there and we have a case," Penny said.

"What about the warrant?" Magee asked.

"The judge is back there reading Lenny's statement now," she responded. "I'll go check." Red Bear said. He came back in a few minutes with the warrant.

"Call Lieutenant Winters and tell him what were about to do. He may want some of his cars in on it since it's in his jurisdiction," Magee told Penny.

Penny made the call and ten minutes later the phone on Bradley Porter's desk in his office in the warehouse rang.

"Yea," Porter said picking up the phone.

"You have about fifteen minutes to get yourself and any records out of there, Magee is about to raid the place," the voice on the phone said.

"Son of a bitch. How did he find us?" Porter asked.

"Those crazy Weams brothers shot one of his deputies. He tracked them down and they're in the county jail. I checked with the judge who issued the warrant. One of them spilled their guts. You better move," the voice said then cut the connection.

Porter went out of his office to the landing at the top of the stairs. He yelled at the few men in the warehouse and then went back inside the office and to a small floor safe. He ran the combination, opened the door and pulled out three ledgers and gathered up the stacks of money shoving them into his suit jacket pockets. Satisfied he had everything he could get away with on such short notice he started down the stairs. He ran as fast as a man his size could, across the warehouse, to a Lincoln parked by one of the overhead doors. He threw the ledgers on the seat, hit the button on the remote control and drove out as the big door opened. He gunned the big car and was two blocks away as the sheriff's cruisers and Pueblo city police cars surrounded the warehouse.

Magee was sure something was wrong when he saw that one of the big overhead doors of the warehouse was open. He drove his cruiser through the door and stopped inside. He slowly got out, not even bothering to draw his weapon. He could see there was no one inside. He walked the length of the large building, heading for the loft in the back. He climbed the stairs to the landing, opened the door and went into the office. The first thing he noticed was the open door of the empty safe. He didn't bother to look around. He turned and went back down to the warehouse floor.

"Run the numbers on the cars and search the office upstairs. I don't think you will find much. Somebody tipped them. They haven't been gone long," he told Penny.

"Call the D.A. too. Ask him to come down here," Magee said.

They looked all through the warehouse, amazed at the number of new automobiles inside. Two car carrier semis sat along one wall near the back of the building. Both were loaded with new Cadillacs and Lincolns.

Walter Sugden, the district attorney, came through the large open door looking for Magee. When he spotted him, he charged across the floor, fire in his eyes.

"Just when did you decide to leave me out of something this big?" he shouted.

"Now don't get all bent out of shape Walter. We got a tip from a not too reliable source. This could have been an empty warehouse," Magee told him.

"You evidently convinced a judge to get a warrant. What have you found?" He said, anger still in his voice.

"Every car in here is hot. There must be at least thirty cars lying around here in just parts. There are two closed semis back there full of parts, ready to ship out. This is a pretty busy chop shop," Magee told him.

"Well write it up and see that I get copies of everything. Who owns the place?" the D.A. said.

"Now that is the surprising thing. The building is in Bradley Porter's name. He was pretty arrogant to think he would never be caught. We'll have a warrant for him as soon as we get everything inventoried. We called Winters. He didn't come along but sent three cars. We'll call him again. The city can impound everything and make it their case if they want it," Magee said.

"I'll talk to the chief and let him decide," the D.A. said and then turned and went out of the building. Penny walked up to Magee, staring at Sugden as he left.

"What got him so excited?" she asked.

"I don't know. This isn't the first time we worked this way. He seemed to be pissed that we raided the place," Magee responded. "Leave some people to seal the place up. Let's get out of here."

Chapter 13

3:00 p.m. Saturday
District Attorney's Office

District Attorney Walter Sugden sat behind his desk waiting for the other three members of his group of conspirators. When he returned to his office from the warehouse where the sheriff was, he made a call to Winters, Morrison and Nash and told them to come to his office for a meeting. Winters was aware of what was bothering him but Morrison and Nash wanted to know what it was about. He had been short with them and told them to just come over. He tried to calm himself as he waited for them. He left his chair and went into his private bathroom where he had a cupboard built into one wall. He opened the two doors and took down a bottle of scotch. He poured a healthy amount in a glass, put the bottle back and drank the liquor down neat. He felt better as the raw whisky warmed his insides. He shut the cupboard doors and went back to his desk. His intercom buzzed, his secretary telling him his peers were here. All three of them came in and found a chair. Nash went to the bathroom and to the liquor cupboard he knew was there. He brought four glasses and a large bottle of bourbon back and proceeded to pour some of Sugden's liquor for each of them. When he finished and sat down, Sugden began.

"Magee just raided the warehouse. Now before you say anything about why he is still alive, you should know that it's been less than a week since I put the contract out. I never question how or when the individual completes a contract, but I did make an exception and call about the delay.

Magee has been in the sheriff's station or surrounded by a dozen deputies. I was told it will take a little longer than usual but was also assured that it will be done," the D.A. told them.

"What about the operation in the warehouse. We need to relocate and get some place going soon. We'll have a back up of merchandise. It would take days to stop the pipeline coming in," Morrison said.

"The family people I know have already agreed to handle things for us for a short time," Nash said. "They have a warehouse in the springs that will accommodate the operation. Aaron has already put the word out."

"What about Porter?" Lieutenant Winters asked.

"Magee will have a warrant for him by now. Where did he go?" the D.A. asked.

"I would bet he lit out for Mexico to hide out," Morrison responded. "Will he talk?"

"We can't take the chance. I'll expand our contract to two," the D.A. said.

The four sat drinking the D.A.'s whiskey and left before suppertime.

Magee was still in his office, trying to figure out who tipped off the people at the warehouse. He wondered about where Bradley Porter would go. He looked through his phone index and found the number for Michael Enserro. He placed the call and a woman answered it. She said the sergeant was not available but she would leave a message for him to return the sheriff's call. Magee figured there wasn't much more he could do this day. He left the office and drove out to the ranch.

He found Helen Little Crow in the kitchen frying chicken for supper. He took a beer from the refrigerator and sat down at the kitchen table.

"When you going to take that girl out on a real date?" Helen asked him.

"What?"

"Penny Booker. When you going to ask her out?"

"You think she would go out with an old reprobate like me?"

"Why not. She thinks a lot of you!"

"How do you figure?"

"The way she looks at you. The way her eyes follow you when you're around her. Any fool could tell."

"I kid her about getting something going between us but she puts me off."

"You sure she puts you off."

"She responds to every thing I say about her."

"She's just sparring. You ask her straight out and see what happens."

Magee sat looking at her, then stood up and went to the phone. He dialed Penny's number. When she answered he hesitated, then spoke.

"Would you like to come out here for dinner tomorrow. Afterward, maybe we could go for a ride on a couple of Little Crow's horses," he said.

"When I heard your voice, I was sure you had some more work for us. Yes, I'd be happy to come for dinner. Does Helen know about this?" Penny asked him.

"She's standing right here," he responded.

"I'll be there. Let's hope everything keeps for Sunday. See you in the morning," she said and hung up.

Helen smiled at him. She didn't ask what Penny said. She knew what she said. Magee took his beer and went outside. The evening was cool but he thought winter was past. He sat down in the swing on the front porch and watched the sun dropping toward the horizon off behind the mountains. Little Crow came up from the barn and sat down on the porch. They sat there watching the sun set, neither saying a word.

Helen called them in for supper and they spent a quiet evening in the living room of the old ranch house.

Magee slept late on Sunday morning. Penny was in the kitchen talking with Helen long before he got up.

"When are you going to get a real relationship started with the sheriff?" Helen asked Penny as she fixed her some breakfast.

"What do you mean, we get along great at work!"

"You know what I mean, something serious on a personal level. You like him don't you?"

"Oh yes. I think he's special."

"Well, why don't you tell him?"

"I'm not sure he feels the same way."

"Trust me, he's been attracted to you from the first time he saw you."

"How do you know?"

"The way he looks at you. The way he watches you when he's with you. I know!"

"It could be difficult, working with him and trying to keep things on a professional level."

"You will never know if you don't try," Helen said.

"Try what?" Magee said as he came into the kitchen, hearing the last of their conversation.

"Good morning," Penny said, slightly embarrassed that he might have heard their conversation.

"You're up early this morning," he responded.

"The thought of getting some of Helen's home cooked food was a good reason to get out here early," she responded.

"Sit down. Your breakfast will be ready soon," Helen told him.

The early morning was cool outside, but the sky was clear and the sun would soon warm the day.

The ranch house was situated on a level plateau with pasture surrounding it on three sides. A quarter mile to the west, the ground rose in a semicircle to a ridge running over a mile. Along the ridge were several groups of trees. Not thick growth as one would find closer to the mountains, but ten to twenty trees of different kinds.

A light green Ford Explorer sat near one group of scrub trees. The trees were few and not very tall, but afforded enough cover to hide the vehicle.

The driver sat in the front seat, the door hanging open. The ranch house was being watched with a pair of high power binoculars.

The Ford was there when Penny drove up to the ranch. The driver watched her vehicle as it left the highway and drove into the front yard. The driver was the individual hired by the district attorney to kill Sheriff Jerico Magee.

Across the sloping pasture, back at the ranch house, Penny and Magee left the kitchen and walked out on the front porch. Charlie Little Crow came walking across the yard leading two horses.

"I hope these are the gentle ones?" Magee said.

"These are the nicest quarter horses in the country," he responded. He held onto the reins as each of them put their foot in the stirrup and crawled up into the saddle. He handed them the reins and stood back. The horses were indeed gentle and responded to the slightest indication that the riders wanted to move. They walked across the yard, through an open gate leading out to the pasture, and then sensing it was to be a slow easy ride, settled into a nice even trot.

The driver of the Explorer was pleased to see them coming across the pasture toward the west, toward the group of trees. He picked up the rifle from the front seat. He leaned across the hood of the vehicle, placing one eye on the scope. The rifle was an AR-16 fitted with a scope and a noise suppresser. He thought about taking the silencer off as he was out in the middle of nowhere. What difference would it make if anyone heard the noise. He decided to leave it on, thinking it would be more of a shock for the sheriff to feel the bullets strike him and not hear any report from the gun that killed him. He patiently waited as the two riders came closer. He had Magee in the scope as he rose up and down with the motion of the horse.

He put his finger on the trigger and was about to apply pressure when he felt hard metal against his left temple. A sudden stab of fear went through his body. His eyes moved to his left searching for what was touching him. He could see the barrel of an automatic pistol.

"Just lay the rifle on the hood and stand up straight. You even blink and I'll splatter your brains all over this nice vehicle," Jimmy Red Bear said to the man. The assassin did as he was told. He released his hold on the rifle and stood up. Red Bear grabbed his left hand, pulling it up behind his back. He snapped handcuffs on his wrist, pulled his right hand back and put the other wrist in the cuffs. He stepped back and took a portable radio from his coat pocket.

"Sheriff 6 to sheriff 2," he said.

Penny reined in her horse. She took a small portable radio from her coat and responded. Magee pulled his horse to a stop and turned to see what she was doing.

"Sheriff 2, go ahead Jimmy," he heard her say.

"A hundred yards straight ahead of you, among the trees," Jimmy Red Bear spoke into his radio.

"I see you now," Penny responded. She touched her horse with her boot heals and he started ahead again. Magee had no idea what she was doing, but started his horse following her. She rode to where Red Bear was and dismounted. Magee came up behind and did the same.

"What's going on Jimmy?" Magee asked, walking toward him and his prisoner.

"This guy was waiting for you to get close enough to blow you away," Red Bear said, pointing at the rifle."

"You just happened to be going by and spotted him?" Magee answered.

"Don't give me hell boss. It was orders from the chief deputy. We picked up on the word there was a contract out on you. We've been screening your back for the past couple days?" Red Bear said.

"Who are we?" Magee asked.

"Me, Reddinger, Reese and Littig. You want me to call Reese over?" he asked Penny. She nodded her head and turned to look at Magee.

"If we told you about keeping an eye on you, you wouldn't have agreed. So don't be upset. This guy could have knocked you off that horse pretty easy from this distance. Who is he Jimmy?" Penny asked.

Red Bear finished talking on his radio then turned to respond.

"Never saw him before. We'll have to have a conversation with him and find out," Red Bear responded. They heard the roar of a car engine off to the south and saw one of the departments four wheel drive vehicles coming across the prairie grass at a pretty good speed. Freddy Reese slid the vehicle to a stop near the trees. He came out of the vehicle, his automatic in his hand. When he saw the prisoner in cuffs, he put his gun away.

"You two had any breakfast?" Magee asked them.

"A little coffee, but if that is an offer, I'm starved," Reese told him.

"Put this guy in the car and take him up to the ranch. Impound the rifle. We'll need to check and see if it was used in any of our open homicides. Ask Helen about something to eat when you get up there," Magee told them.

"You want a wrecker for the Ford?" Red Bear asked.

"No. I think we're going to keep this one real quiet for a while. You drive it to the yard. The chief deputy and I are going to finish our ride then we'll be along. Lock this guy up somewhere until you've eaten, then see who he is and anything else he will tell you," Magee said as he put his foot in the stirrup and mounted the horse. Penny watched as Reese put the prisoner in his vehicle and Red Bear got in the Ford. She mounted her horse and walked him up beside Magee as the two vehicles drove off across the open pasture.

"If I had told you, we would never have caught this one?" Penny said.

"It's all right. I'm impressed that you could screen me without my knowing it. I must be getting old," he said, grinning at her. He started his horse walking and her horse fell in beside.

"Jimmy and Reese took one shift, then Reddinger and Littig relieved them. It was not easy for Jimmy to sneak up on this guy as open as this country is," she said.

"Ah yes, but remember, he has the blood of his ancestors running through his veins. The guy didn't have a chance. Who do you figure hired him?" Magee asked.

"Maybe we can get him to tell us," she responded.

"He ruined our ride didn't he?"

"Yes!"

"You're anxious to go back and make him talk?"

"Yes!"

"Then let's do it," he responded turning his horse toward the ranch house.

They rode back across the open prairie and to the corral by the barn. Little Crow met them and took the horses. They walked to the house and went into the kitchen. Red Bear and Reese were at the kitchen table waiting for Helen to put the food on the table.

"Where'd you put him?" Penny asked.

"He's locked in the pump house out back," Red Bear responded. "We found this on him," he continued pointing at the few items lying on the sideboard.

Penny picked up the man's wallet, opening it. She found a driver's license issued in the State of Missouri. There was a money clip with a few twenties, a pocketknife and a pack of cigarettes and a lighter. The license said he was Lester Steen with a Kansas City address. He was thirty-one, weighed one seventy, had blue green eyes and was five eleven. The picture appeared to be that of the prisoner.

Magee followed her as she went out the back door then to the small wooden structure where the prisoner was locked in. She pulled the peg from the hasp on the door and went inside. Steen was sitting on the concrete floor, his hands still cuffed behind his back. She grabbed his shoulder on one side, Magee grabbed the other and they pulled him up on his feet. Magee shoved him through the door and they took him into the living room.

They put him on a straight back wooden chair in front of a large oval table and sat down on each side of him.

"You want Red Bear and Reese to run him to the station and book him when they're finished eating?" she asked Magee.

"No, I think we'll do this one different. I don't expect he will talk without some assistance. I think Little Crow and Red Bear can take him out to the barn and peel his skin off until he tells us what we want to know," Magee said.

"Well then we won't be able to use what he says in court," she responded.

"We can get by without his testimony. I doubt if he knows very much. He's just hired help. He's no pro. If he killed for a living, we wouldn't have taken him so easy. Let's see. We have the late Sheriff Orville Boone that was murdered, three deputies, Everett Cline, Joe Black, Glenn Dunn and the state trooper. The kid that boosted cars they found floating in the river and Eldon Jones hanging in his jail cell. That's eight murders all connected to big time criminals working our county. I doubt if he killed any of them. When Red Bear and Little Crow get through with him, talk or not, have him taken over to Bill Nash in Ouster County. He can put him in a cell there to rot. No one will think of looking for him there," Magee said.

"He doesn't get an attorney then?" Penny responded.

"Well, I guess that will depend on whether he lives through the interrogation. I'll go get the boys to start working on him!" Magee said getting up from his chair.

"Hold it," Steen said. "Hold on a minute."

"Well he can talk," Penny said.

"The sheriff is right. I didn't kill none of those people," Steen said.

"Well you weren't out here hunting pheasants. We have you on conspiracy to commit murder," Penny said.

"I didn't have a hell of a lot of choice. I was told to do it. A guy hasn't got much choice. When they tell you to do something, you better do it," Steen said.

"Who told you to do it?" Magee asked.

"Sugden. Walter Sugden," he responded.

"Walter Sugden!" Penny said with surprise. "The district attorney?"

"That's the guy. I don't usually work direct for him, but Porter took off."

"You work for Bradley Porter?" Magee asked.

"Yea. I was one of the guys that made sure everything ran okay stripping down the cars they brought in. Me and a couple of the other guys would use a little muscle if any of the other people got out of line. Porter told us Sugden and his buddies hired a pro from back east to take out Orville Boone. I guess that is who did all the others too," Steen told them.

"Walter Sugden called you and told you to kill me," Magee asked him.

"He didn't ask. He told me to do it."

"You said Sugden and his buddies. Who are his buddies?" Penny asked.

"The guys that run everything. Chief Morrison, that guy Winters who works for him and the lawyer, Art Nash," he told them.

"That would explain who tipped off Porter about the raid on the hot car warehouse. I called Winters to include the police department in on the deal," Magee said. "The hard part to accept is Walt Sugden. Hell, he gave my name to the county board for this job!"

"Call someone out here to get his statement down on paper. When he's finished, we will take him over for Bill Nash to keep for us. We need to talk to the attorney general about this. It will take his help to get all these heavy hitters in jail," Magee said.

Helen Little Crow interrupted them to tell Magee he had a phone call. He left the room and picked up the call in the kitchen.

"Good morning Jerry. I received the message to call you," Sergeant Michael Enserro said.

"Thank you for calling back. We have a felony warrant out for a guy named Bradley Porter. He may have come over your border to hide out. Is there a fax number I can send you a copy of the warrant and information on the guy?" Magee asked.

"We'll help all we can," Enserro said. He gave Magee the number. "Any idea where he may have come across?" Enserro continued.

"I would guess near El Paso, Texas. Let me know if you locate him," Magee said then put the phone down. He went back to the living room where Red Bear, Reese, Little Crow, Penny and the prisoner were all together. Penny was giving the deputies instructions on what to do with Steen. When she finished she walked over to Magee.

"We can put enough together to get a warrant for Sugden and his buddies on everything but the murders. We still have to find the pro Steen was talking about," Penny said.

"Porter may know something if we can find him," Magee said. He told her about his call from Enserro. He gave her the fax number and she went to the phone to call the dispatcher and told her what to send to the Mexican National Police.

A stenographer came to the ranch and she sat down to record Steen's statement as Penny led him through it. They finished just before lunch and Red Bear and Reese transported Steen to the Ouster County jail. Helen called everyone in for lunch and they sat down around the kitchen table.

In Pueblo, District Attorney Walter Sugden was eating his lunch at an expensive restaurant down town. He was halfway through the meal when his portable cellular phone rang. When he answered it, he immediately recognized the voice of the professional killer.

"Why did you send one of Porter's men after the sheriff?" the voice asked him.

"I had pressure to get the job done. You were getting nowhere," Sugden responded.

"That was a mistake. When I am given a contract, it is not given to someone else. I consider the contract void. I also repute the contract on Porter. You find someone who doesn't care if you play games with them," the killer said.

"You can't get out of this that easy. You're in this as deep as any of us. You finish the deal or,"

"Or what?" he was interrupted. "Don't threaten me. The last person that hired me, and then threatened me, is no longer breathing. You got your moneys worth on the others. You can finish it yourself. Don't try to contact me again." The phone went dead. Sugden swore, throwing the phone down on the table. He picked up the glass of wine on the table and drank it down. His stomach churned, ruining the rest of his meal. He would have to eliminate the pro. Now how do you go about killing a professional killer he wondered?

At the ranch, Penny and Magee finished eating then drove to the station in the city. Magee went to his office and placed a call to the attorney general in Denver. He found him at home and spent an hour on the phone with him. He told Magee he would send two of his deputies to Pueblo on Monday morning to gather up the evidence and plan a course of action. As soon as Magee put the phone down the dispatcher told him he had a call from Mexico.

"We found Porter," Michael Enserro told him. "He's holed up in an expensive hotel in Mexico City. You want us to take him?"

"Go ahead and pick him up. We'll come down and talk to him. Where should we come to?" Magee asked. Enserro gave him the location of the federal building but told him not to worry. When he arrived at the airport he would have a car meet him and take him to the place. Magee thanked him and hung up. He left the office to look for Penny. He found her at her desk going over active cases.

"I ask you out for a day off. When I called you said you wondered about the call being work and here we are sucked back into working on Saturday. Want to go for a ride?" he asked her, and then told her about his phone call from Enserro. "Do you know where we can charter a plane for the trip?"

"I don't but Emma will know who to call. I'll check with her," Penny said picking up the phone. She called Emma at home and got the name of a charter service. She placed the call and hired a plane for the trip to Mexico City.

Less than an hour later, she and Magee were walking across the apron at the airport to a small Citation business jet. The pilot and an attendant met them at the door of the plane. Fifteen minutes later, they were in the air heading south. Two hours later they were walking through the front door of a federal police station in the Mexican capital city. Sergeant Michael Enserro met them in the lobby.

"It is good to see you sheriff. Welcome Deputy Booker he said to Penny as he shook both their hands. We have Porter upstairs in an interrogation room. Will you need a stenographer?" Enserro asked.

"Thank you yes. We might as well get it down from the start," Magee said. They followed Enserro to an elevator, then to a small room on the second floor. Porter sat at a table in the room, a uniformed guard stood near the wall. Penny and Magee were a little shocked at the size of the man. They were also surprised at how expensively he was dressed.

"Porter, this is Chief Deputy Penny Booker and I am Jerry Magee. We're with the Pueblo County Sheriff's Department," Magee told him as they pulled out a chair and sat down.

"I know who you are Magee. I want my attorney present if this is going to be a formal interview and I want to talk about making a deal," Porter said.

"Well now whom would you make a deal with. The district attorney of the jurisdiction you committed most of your crimes in is about to be arrested for his own crimes," Penny said.

"So, you know about Sugden. What about the rest of his board of directors," Porter asked.

"We have most of it Porter. One of your enforcers, Lester Steen is under arrest and gave us quite a statement," Magee said.

"Well, then my list of things to trade has suddenly become much smaller," Porter responded.

"What do you know about the professional hit man Sugden hired?" Penny asked.

"It isn't a man. I don't know who it is but I'm sure it's a woman," Porter said.

"How do you know that?" Magee asked.

"The district attorney let it slip once. He was unhappy when the sheriff was found dead in a motel. He said the bitch could have found a better place to kill him. He didn't know I heard him say that," Porter told them.

"You're indictment will be handled by the state attorney general. I don't even know the man. You will have to make any deals with him," Magee told him. "We will start extradition proceedings on Monday. You should be back in Pueblo by the end of next week. By the way, what are the chances of Sugden sending the woman after you when he finds out you have been caught."

"I would say that possibility is certain. You provide me very tight security and I shall tell all I know," Porter said.

"Could we have that stenographer now?" Penny asked Enserro.

"Of course. This turned out easier than you thought," Enserro said as he left the room. He came back with a woman who set up and started recording Porter's statement as Penny and Magee walked him through everything beginning with Orville Boone's murder. It was past dark when they finished. Porter was taken to a cell. Enserro told them he had taken the liberty of booking a room in a hotel for them. He said he would invite them to his home but he didn't live here in Mexico City. He took them downstairs to a waiting police car and they thanked him for his help and were driven across the city to the hotel.

They were escorted into the lobby and were in awe of how lavish the place was. It had to be a very expensive hotel. The policeman escorting them went to the desk and registered them, telling the concierge that they were guests of the Mexican government. They were escorted to the elevator and then to a suite of rooms on the top floor of the building.

The suite was huge, with two bedrooms, a large living room, two bathrooms, a kitchen and a terrace overlooking the city. When they were alone Magee picked up the phone and called room service.

When the call was answered, he handed the phone to Penny and asked her to order them supper. He went to one of the bathrooms and started taking off his clothes. He found shaving supplies in a medicine chest and was soaping up his face when Penny came into the room.

"We're lucky Enserro put us up here since we didn't bring any luggage. This place probably has everything we need," he said. He was just a little shy about standing in front of her wearing nothing but his brief shorts as he shaved. This shyness soon left him as he watched her in the mirror. She turned on the water in the bathtub and started undressing behind him. He was pleasantly surprised when she was down to her underwear and didn't hesitate for a second. Her bra then her panties came off. She stepped into the tub, found a washcloth and soap and started scrubbing.

He couldn't take his eyes off her breasts. They were beautiful, firm mounds of lovely flesh with red nipples, hard as ice. He finished shaving, pulled his shorts down and stepped out of them. He climbed into the tub facing her. She twisted around in the tub until her back was to him. She handed him the washcloth, all lathered up with soap. He knew she wanted him to wash her back. He slowly scrubbed it until the skin was bright pink. When he finished she stood up, stepped out of the tub then got back in behind him, scooting him down until there was room for her to get in. She took the washcloth and scrubbed his back. When she was finished, she reached around his waist and took his growing hard on in her hand. He leaned back against her hard breasts, pushing his hips up into her hand.

"It took us long enough to get here," she said.

"You are as beautiful as I saw you in my fantasies," he said.

"You had fantasies too?"

"You know it. I imagined how you looked without your clothes every time I saw you," he said.

"I guess I never took you serious enough. I've thought about this too, you know. You're bigger than I imagined though. I wonder if I can accommodate this," she said.

"Lets find out," he said as he stood up, turned and pulled her up with him. They stepped out of the tub and dried each other with a large towel. He took her hand and led her to the big bed, pulling down the covers; he gently pushed her down on the cool silk sheets. He leaned forward to kiss her and they became lost in each other for most of the night. It was almost dawn when they fell into an exhausted sleep.

Enserro provided them transportation to the airport on Sunday morning. They flew back to Pueblo and drove to the sheriff's station. Magee went to his office and when Penny came in later, he told her to go on home and he would come by after he had his work finished. After she left, he picked up the phone and called his snitch, Virgil Dykes. He talked to him a few minutes, and then hung up. He placed a call to the airport in Denver, then hurried out to his car and squealed the tires on the concrete as he left the parking lot. He drove to the interstate and was well over the speed limit when he came up the on ramp and blended in with the traffic headed north.

It was one hundred and six miles to the Denver airport. He made it in an hour and forty minutes in heavy traffic. He wound around through the terminal looking for the airline he wanted. He parked in a red zone and left the car. He hurried into the terminal and stopped by the electronic board looking for a flight destination and time of departure. Good he had twenty minutes yet. He looked all around the airline desk, and then went to the departure gate. Nothing. He went back out in front and stood by the door looking all around the parking lots. Fifty yards away he spotted her getting out of a car. She was on the far side of the lot. He hurried across the street and into the lot. When he was about to her, Maddie Patterson spotted him. She stopped, and just stood there, holding a bag in each hand, her face white as a sheet.

"Hi Maddie. Set the bags down, then put your purse down with them," he said to her as he pulled his automatic out.

"Jerry. What are you doing here," she said, some of the color returning to her face.

"I know who you are Maddie and what you do for a living. Set the bags down, then take the purse off your shoulder and set it down," he repeated.

She set the bags on the concrete and slowly straightened up. He was about to tell her again about the purse when a man's voice behind him yelled "freeze!" He looked out of the corner of his eye and saw an airport policeman holding a gun on him.

"Put the gun down, now!" the policeman yelled.

"I'm a policeman too, making a felony arrest," Magee yelled back at him.

"I said put the gun down, God damn it," the policeman yelled. He appeared to be very excited. Magee could see this was going nowhere. He slowly bent over to put his automatic on the ground. Maddie immediately opened her purse and came out with a gun in her hand. She brought it up to fire when he heard the report of an automatic very close by. Maddie was hit in the chest with two thuds, the impact of the bullets driving her back. Magee reached down and retrieved his weapon but it wasn't needed. He turned to his left and twenty feet away stood Deputy Sheriff Penny Booker, her automatic still in both hands, aiming at where she had just fired. He turned back to look for the airport policeman. Deputy James Red Bear was standing with his automatic under the man's chin. He was holding the policeman's weapon in his left hand.

Magee slowly put his gun away and walked the few feet to where Maddie lay on the concrete. He felt her neck for a pulse then took his fingers and pulled the eyelids down over the open, unseeing eyes.

"You sure led us a chase down the interstate," Penny said as she put her weapon away.

"Why didn't you call and tell me you two were behind me?" he said.

"We tried. No response. You're radio must not be working," she said.

"I'm damn glad I didn't lose you in the traffic. I believe she would have gotten me," Magee said.

"How did you know it was her and how did you find her?" Red Bear said as he came up behind them. The officer wasn't saying a thing. Red Bear had him scared to speak.

"I really had nothing but a hunch. She was around every time we came up with a dead body. She was always supposed to be representing one of the crooks. We all saw her with Sugden several times. I had the idea she was always lying to me. I called Virgil Dykes when we got back and he confirmed there was a woman from back east in this line of work. I called the airlines and was surprised when I found out she used the name Margaret Patterson when she booked the flight. The look on her face when I saw her here was all the proof I needed. How did you two get behind me?" he asked.

"I was leaving the building when Red Cloud almost ran me down with his car. He said you took off out of there like a bat out of hell. He was still covering you. I jumped in with him and tried several times to call you on the radio. We were almost here before we figured you were going to the airport. We spotted her about the same time you did," Penny said.

"Officer, I am Sheriff Jerico Magee from Pueblo. These are two of my deputies. We were after this woman for murder. She was about to leave on a plane," Magee told the policeman. "Give him back his gun, Red Bear. Now if you will call it in I think we need some local detectives and a coroner out here."

The frightened officer took the gun and took a portable radio from his belt. He spoke into it and in a few minutes, officers came from everywhere. Magee leaned back against the fender of a car and lit a cigarette. They spent two hours in the lot then went across the city to a police station and spent another three hours with the investigating officers.

When they were free to go, Penny told Red Bear she would ride back with Magee. They were soon back on the interstate headed south.

"I think we should get married," Magee said.

"Oh you do. You like me enough to want to marry me," she teased him.

"Well, that too, but if we were married, I would know where you were all the time," he teased her right back. "Oh, and please make the wedding plain and simple."

Penny Booker and Jerico Magee were married the first Sunday in March. The wedding was in a large old cathedral in Pueblo and the reception was out at the big old ranch house. There were over four hundred in attendance.

The day after they returned from Denver, the attorney general's people came to Pueblo and spent a week getting the evidence lined up then participated in the arrest of the police chief, the chief of detectives and the district attorney along with the prominent lawyer Arthur Nash. A grand jury was convened that week and several indictments were brought against everyone involved. The coroner's inquest into Margaret Patterson's death was ruled justifiable during a lawful arrest.

The newly weds took a week off and traveled to the gulf at Brownsville and rented a beach house. They were seen very little outside the house all week.

9 780595 093298

Printed in Great Britain
by Amazon

21205005R00109